Hit and Run

Dawn Hunter
and
Karen Hunter

James Lorimer & Company Ltd., Publishers
Toronto, 1999

First publication in the United States, 1999

James Lorimer & Company Ltd. acknowledges the support of the Department of Canadian Heritage and the Ontario Arts Council in the development of writing and publishing in Canada. We acknowledge the support of the Canada Council for the Arts for our publishing program.

Cover illustration: Greg Ruhl   Canadä

Canadian Cataloguing in Publication Data
Hunter, Dawn
    Hit and run
(Sports series)
ISBN 1-55028-673-0 (bound)   ISBN 1-55028-672-2 (pbk.)

I. Hunter, Karen, 1960-   II. Title. III. Series: Sports stories
(Toronto, Ont)
PS8565.U5784H57 1999   jC813'.54   C99-930337-6
PZ7.H86Hi 1999

James Lorimer & Company Ltd.,   Distributed in the United States by:
Publishers   Orca Book Publishers
35 Britain Street   P.O. Box 468
Toronto, Ontario   Custer, WA USA
M5A 1R7   98240–0468

Printed and bound in Canada.

Contents

To our mother, Mary, who taught us that we could;
To our father, Tom, who believed that we would;
To Judith and Jean, who told us that we should;
To Roger and Peter, who made sure that we did;
And especially to Adam, the reason for it all.

1

Warming Up

Quit pushing me. I'm trying to see the list!" Glen Thomson planted himself firmly in front of the East York Community Centre's bulletin board. He wanted to be the first to know who had made this year's little league team.

"We're all trying to see the list. Just because you're taller doesn't mean you can hog the space," Ravi Singh exclaimed, peering over Glen's shoulder.

"Chill, Ravi," Jacob Collins laid a hand on the other boy's shoulder. "It's not going anywhere. We'll all get a chance to see it."

The boys clustered around the bulletin board had all tried out for the East York Eagles. Now, after weeks of anticipation, the final list had been posted. Glen had his fingers crossed that he and Jacob would be playing ball together this summer. Last year, neither boy had made the team, and Glen knew that his dad had been disappointed.

The boys had worked hard to improve their baseball skills over the last few months and were hoping the extra effort had paid off. Glen and Jacob did everything together ever since Glen and his family had moved into the neighbourhood three years ago.

"Is my name there?" Derek Langley asked from the back of the group.

Glen scanned the list. "Sorry, Derek. You didn't make it," he said quickly. "But Jacob and I did!"

"We did? All right!" Jacob high-fived his friend. "This is going to be an awesome summer!"

"Congratulations, guys," Derek said quietly.

Jacob turned to the disappointed boy. "Don't worry, man. There's always next year," he said. "Glen and I didn't make it last year, when we were ten. Right, Glen?"

"What?" Glen was daydreaming about the summer ahead. "I didn't hear you." He was already winning the championship in his mind.

"I was telling Derek that he'll make it next year too, if he practises hard."

"Oh, yeah. Don't feel too bad, Derek. We'll try out all together next year." Glen made his way towards the front door. "Come on, Jacob, let's go. I've got to be home before dinner."

Stepping out into the bright June sunshine, the boys squinted, fumbling for their sunglasses. Glen pushed his shock of straight blond hair out of his eyes, adjusting his new sunglasses and posing.

"Hey, where'd you get the shades?" Jacob raised his eyebrows, noticing the expensive brand name.

"My father sent 'em to me. Everyone in California is wearing them."

Glen's father had been living in California since his parents had divorced three years ago. Though Glen rarely saw his dad, they kept in touch by phone. At least once a month, cards and presents arrived for Glen and his older brother, Joshua. Glen thought that the presents were cool, but he wished that his dad could deliver them in person. He had been devastated when his dad had told him that he was moving so far away.

"Make sure you get a cheap pair for ball," Jacob said. "You don't want to lose them!"

As the boys walked up Pape Avenue, they excitedly discussed the summer ahead.

"I'm going to hit more home runs than McGwire this year," Glen bragged.

"Get real," Jacob laughed. "You'll be lucky to get off the bench."

"No way! I just know I'm going to be a star." Glen held his clenched fist above his head, mimicking a victory lap around the bases.

"I hope that my parents make it out to some games," Jacob said. "They don't really understand baseball that much. 'In the Caribbean, we all played soccer and cricket. Why don't you play soccer?'"

Glen laughed at Jacob's imitation of his father's deep voice and thick Barbadian accent. Secretly he hoped that he really would be a star player. Maybe then his mother would pay more attention to him. It seemed to Glen that, ever since his new stepsister, Megan, had arrived, he had had to compete for his mom's attention. Sharing her was not something he enjoyed. He felt like he had already given up his father, and he wasn't about to give up his mother, too.

The boys parted at Glen's house on Beechwood, a short street in Toronto's east end. The house was typical of the area: two storeys with a big front porch and a maple tree growing in the front yard. Glen loved the view from his bedroom window — the house sat near the edge of the Don Valley ravine. He bounded up the front steps, eager to share his good news. He had noticed that his stepfather Andrew's truck was not parked in the driveway. Good, Glen thought, now I can tell my mom without *him* being there.

Andrew had dated Glen's mom for about two years before they married, and Glen wasn't sure that he liked this new arrangement. He hadn't minded Andrew so much when he and his mom were just dating. Now, it seemed as if Andrew was trying to take his real dad's place, and Glen wasn't sure how he felt about it. Sometimes it was kind of nice to have Andrew around, but he also felt a little disloyal to his own dad. He preferred to keep Andrew at a distance. Bursting into the house, Glen dropped his backpack in the hallway and shouted for his mother.

"In here," Catherine called from the kitchen. "Don't slam the door!"

Glen ran down the short hallway, stopping to hug Jasper, the family's yellow Lab. Glen's dad had given Jasper to him just before he moved to California and the dog had been a great comfort to Glen after he was gone. Glen could tell Jasper anything.

As he hugged Jasper, he whispered the good news in the dog's ear. "Hi, boy! Guess what? I finally made the team." Jasper licked his face and Glen laughed.

Going into the kitchen, Glen saw that Megan was setting the table for dinner. Her dark curly hair fell over her small face as she concentrated on placing the knives and forks correctly. Feeling guilty, Glen realized that it had been his turn to do this. Keeping his news to himself for a few more minutes, he turned to Megan.

"Megan, you didn't have to do that."

"That's okay, Glen," she replied, smiling. "I don't mind helping you."

At six years old, Megan was delighted to have a new mother and two older brothers. Their parents had only been married for four months, and Glen envied how well she had adjusted to the new arrangement.

"Your report came today, Glen." Catherine stood on her tiptoes to retrieve the envelope from the top of the fridge and turned to him. "I'm glad to see you pulled up your mark in English a little."

Glen shrugged. He had tried hard to improve his grades this year, but he knew he'd never be an honour student. Besides, he wanted to talk about baseball, not about school.

"I know you were making more of an effort with your homework, and it looks like it paid off." Catherine handed Glen the report card, tucking a stray blond curl behind her ear. "Maybe in the fall, we should think about getting a tutor."

Glen ran his eyes quickly down the column of grades. He wasn't surprised to see that most of them were in the 60s. The only subject he was good at was gym, and he smiled when he saw the 82 beside it.

"Aw, Mom." Glen folded the report card back into its envelope. "Summer vacation just started. I don't want to think about school right now," he said, handing it back to her.

"Okay, Glen." Catherine put the report card back on top of the fridge. "We can talk about it again in September." She turned back to the salad she had been making. "Josh," Glen's mom said, "can you get that big bowl down from the top shelf for me, please?"

"Sure." Josh unfolded his six-foot frame from the table. He patted the top of his mother's head and she laughed and ducked away.

Walking past Glen, Josh punched him in the shoulder playfully. "You look like you're about to burst. Is there something you want to share?"

Glen's mom turned to look at him again. "You *do* look pretty excited."

"Mom, did you forget that the final cuts for the baseball team were posted today?" Glen asked, a little hurt that she hadn't remembered.

"Oh, Glen, I'm so sorry. I forgot," Catherine apologized. "Did you make it?"

Glen didn't feel as excited as he had in the community centre. "Yeah, I did. Our first practice is this weekend."

ay to go!" Josh said enthusiastically. "I wish I were still playing little league."

"Oh boy, Glen. Can I come and watch you play?" Megan asked, her big brown eyes pleading with Glen.

"We'll see, Megan. I'm not sure anyone else's little sisters are going to be there," Glen replied.

Megan looked down dejectedly.

"Oh, sweetie," Glen's mother said to her, "I'm sure we can all go and watch him play sometimes." She walked over to the little girl and gave her shoulder a squeeze.

"Glen, I'm so proud of you," Catherine said, stepping close to her son for a hug. "I'm sure you're going to be great."

Glen started chattering about the summer ahead, and about how well he was going to play. He was surprised when his mother interrupted him.

"What about Jacob?"

"What about him?" Glen furrowed his brow, wondering what she meant.

"Did he make the team too? You haven't mentioned him at all," his mom said with exasperation.

"Oh," Glen shrugged. "Yeah, he made it too. It'll be fun to play on the same team."

Glen started to tell his mom who else was on the team when he heard the front door close.

"Glen?" Andrew called. "Is this your backpack lying here in the hallway?"

Glen groaned to himself and rolled his eyes. As he was about to answer, his stepfather walked into the kitchen. Andrew took off his baseball hat, grabbed some paper towel and wiped his face. His blue eyes twinkled as he strode over to Catherine and bent down to kiss her cheek. Andrew was very different from Glen's dad, and Glen was still having trouble relating to him.

"Andrew!" she exclaimed. "You're filthy! What kind of job were you on today?"

"We were cleaning eavestroughs that I don't think had ever been emptied before," he laughed. "What a day!" Turning to Glen, Andrew again asked him to go put his backpack away.

Glen couldn't help comparing Andrew to his dad, Bob. Working for a large software developer, his dad was always dressed perfectly. Though Andrew owned his own contracting business, he didn't hesitate to work alongside his employees. Glen couldn't understand that; he had never seen his own dad get dirty — he had always hired other people to clean their eavestroughs.

Thinking back, Glen remembered how it had been when his parents were still married. His dad had rarely been home long enough to do any work around the house. The whole family's time had revolved around his career and his ambitions. His dad had always told Glen that it was important to be the best at whatever you did, no matter what it took.

"I had forgotten you'd be home early tonight, Catherine. What's for dinner?" Andrew asked, putting an arm around her waist. They had a deal that whichever parent was home first took care of dinner.

"I'm trying a new recipe that I want to add to the menu at the café," she replied. "You get to be my guinea pigs again, I'm afraid." Catherine owned a small café on The Danforth, a popular stretch of restaurants and stores in Toronto. She often experimented with new meals at home.

"Don't you want to share your good news with Andrew?" Catherine asked, turning to Glen.

"Oh, yeah. I made the little league team," Glen mumbled. "I gotta go put my backpack away." As he turned to leave, Andrew called him back.

"I'm proud of you, Glen," he said. "I know you worked hard to make the team. When's the first game? I want to make sure I book some time off."

"I'm not sure yet." Glen looked down and scuffed the floor with his toe. "We'll get the schedule this weekend. But don't worry about trying to make my games. I'm sure my mom will be there."

"And me too!" Megan piped up.

"Mom, can I go call Dad and tell him about the team?" Glen asked, turning to leave the kitchen again.

"I think you should wait until after dinner to call him," she replied. "Remember, it's three hours earlier in California and he's probably not home from work yet."

Glen reluctantly agreed. After dinner, it was still a little early to try calling his dad, so Glen decided to catch a few innings of the Blue Jays game on television. The Jays were his favourite team, and Andrew and Joshua both shared his interest. The family settled into the den, just in time to see Carlos Delgado come up to bat with the bases loaded.

"I bet he hits a homer!" Glen said excitedly from his spot on the floor.

"Let's just hope he gets on base," Josh responded. "I haven't seen too many grand slams this year."

From the television screen, a cheer went up from the crowd as Delgado hit the ball after two strikes were called.

"Get out of there!" Glen called to the ball, holding his breath. He let it out a second later as Albert Belle charged out to the warning track and caught the fly ball.

Everyone groaned. "That's all right," Andrew consoled them. "It's early in the game. We can still come back."

Restlessly Glen glanced at the watch his dad had sent him for his birthday. "Can I call Dad now?" he asked his mom.

"Sure, go ahead," she said.

Glen leapt to his feet. "I'm going to use the phone in the kitchen," he said over his shoulder.

He closed the kitchen door and dialled his dad's home phone number. "Hello?" It was Louisa, his dad's housekeeper, on the other end of the line.

"Hi, Louisa. It's Glen," he replied. "Can I talk to my dad, please?"

"I'm sorry, Glen. He's still at the office," she told him. "You know your dad. He's going to be at work for several more hours. Why don't you try him there?"

Glen knew his dad's office number by heart. He dialled, waiting impatiently for his dad to answer.

"Bob Thomson here," his dad said abruptly.

"Hi, Dad!"

"Glen! You just caught me before my dinner meeting. How are you doing, Sport?"

"Good, Dad. Guess what? I made the little league team this year!"

"Oh, wait a minute. Someone's just stepped into my office. I have to put you on hold for a minute."

Glen waited impatiently. His dad was always busy, but Glen supposed it was because he was so important.

"Sorry about that, Glen. Now, what were you saying?"

"I made the baseball team this year."

"That's great! I told you that you hadn't worked hard enough last year. Oh, wait a minute. My other line is ringing."

Conversations with his father always seemed to go like this. Glen was used to sharing his news in little pieces.

"Dad? I know you're busy, but do you think you might be able to come up here this summer and watch me play a game?" Glen hadn't seen his dad in more than a year. Bob had cancelled his last two trips.

"Sure. I think I can arrange a business trip to Toronto in August. How would that be?"

"Great! I can't wait. I'll tell Josh that you're coming. Thanks, Dad."

"Give him my love too, will you? Sorry, Glen but I've got to run. I'll talk to you soon. Love you."

Glen heard his father hang up the phone. He really hoped his dad could keep his promise this time. Going back into the den, Glen shared the news of his father's visit. Out of the corner of his eye, he saw his mom and Andrew exchange a glance.

"Oh, he's gracing us with his presence this summer, is he?" Josh's voice dripped with sarcasm.

"Hey, Josh," Andrew admonished him. "I'm sure he'll do his best to get here. I know that Bob will want to watch Glen play ball."

"Of course he will!" Glen turned on Josh, stung by his words. "Come on Jasper, let's finish watching the game upstairs."

The Jays pulled off a 6-5 victory over the Baltimore Orioles, and Glen had settled into bed. Jasper was curled at his side, where he always slept.

"You know, Jasper, Jacob and I are going to have a great summer. I really hope that I can make pitcher — that's the most important position, you know. My parents would be so proud if I were the pitcher. I know I could do a good job." Jasper wagged his tail as Glen spoke to him. He buried his hand in the dog's thick fur and spoke quietly.

"I just hope that Dad comes this time. I really miss him. I know that he had to cancel before because of work, and I know it's not because he doesn't love me. He would be here if he could. Sometimes I get a little mad at him though. I know Andrew is always here, but it's not the same." Glen sighed. "He's not my real dad." Glen turned over, hugged Jasper tightly, and closed his eyes.

2

Tryouts

"Why don't we stop here, Glen, and walk the bikes down the hill?" Jacob asked as the boys neared Riverdale Park. They were on their way to the first team practice for the East York Eagles. They both looked longingly at the swimming pool, knowing that there wouldn't be much time for swimming this summer.

Nearing the bottom of the steep hill, the two boys saw that most of their teammates had already arrived on the baseball diamond. Nick and Maurice, two of the boys Glen knew from school, were playing catch. Ravi and a small blond-haired boy were doing some warm-up stretches under the trees that grew along the fence.

"Hey, Ravi!" Jacob called.

"Hi, guys!" Ravi shot them a friendly smile and waved them over. "Come and meet my friend, Steve Matthews."

Glen dug Jacob in the ribs with his elbow. "Boy! How did that guy ever make the team?" he whispered.

Steve was short and slight. Glen wasn't sure he'd be strong enough to pick up the bat.

"Glen!" Jacob whispered back. "That's mean. He's not that small. After all, he had to try out too. He must be a good player." They wheeled their bikes over to the fence and locked them.

"Hi," Steve said, smiling. "What a cool bike."

"Thanks. My dad gave it to me," Glen replied, thinking that maybe this kid wasn't so bad after all.

"Guys? Can I have your attention please?" the coach asked.

Tom Johnson, the team's coach, ran his eyes over the clipboard he was holding. He was a man in his late forties with grown-up children, who enjoyed keeping active by coaching little league. Removing his glasses, the coach wiped the sweat from his face.

"It sure is hot, isn't it?" he said. "I won't work you too hard today. We'll spend some time getting to know each other, and I will assign your playing positions for the season. We'll keep the practice short for the first day. Now, when I call your name, please raise your hand."

As the coach called out the names, Glen glanced at his teammates. He already knew Maurice Lavoie and Nick Apidopoulos, but not all the boys had tried out at the same time. Glen tried to remember how well the other boys had pitched during tryouts. Glen was sure that he would be one of the three chosen to pitch.

"Michael Wong?" the coach called. The boy who raised his hand was one whom Glen remembered well. He had a really good arm, and his tryout pitches had been fast. He certainly posed some competition for Glen.

"Kamal Warner?" A tall boy raised his hand shyly. He stood at the back of the group and hadn't spoken to anyone so far. Glen mentally dismissed him.

Coach Johnson continued through the list of names, and Glen sized up each boy in turn. Marco Nelson was a strong-looking boy with black curly hair and dark eyes. He had done really well at the tryouts and could play any position.

The chubby boy who answered to the name Miguel Keys looked to Glen like he might have some power at the plate. Chris Sanders couldn't seem to keep his glasses on his nose, and Ken Nakamura could hardly stand still long enough for the coach to finish the role call.

"Where's Ryan Parks? He's the only one we're missing." Coach Johnson scanned the diamond and the surrounding field.

"He's never on time for anything," Glen replied. Ryan had been in Glen's class last year. Everyone had always teased him about his red hair and freckles, but Ryan handled it well. He and Glen had worked on a science project together, and Ryan had been a lot of fun, but late for everything.

Just then Ryan came charging down the hill.

"I'm sorry I'm late," he was yelling, before he had even reached them. "I couldn't find my glove and my shoelace broke, and —"

"We don't need the excuses, Ryan," the coach interrupted. "But we do need you to be on time for practices and games. A team relies on all its players equally."

Ryan looked at the ground. "I'll be on time from now on."

Coach Johnson sent them to run a lap around the track to get them warmed up.

"That Steve is pretty fast, isn't he?" Jacob panted to Glen when they were finished. "He'll be great at running bases."

"Yeah," Glen replied, "but he's too puny to hit any home runs."

The practice began in earnest with Coach Johnson pitching to each boy in turn. He tried to encourage them and explain how to improve their skills, rather than criticize them. Glen watched each of the other players and decided that he could impress the coach. He was better than most of them.

"Keep the bat off your shoulder, Kamal. You have to swing like you mean it." Although Kamal hadn't said much, he seemed to listen carefully to everything the coach said. He had only been in Canada for a short time and seemed self-conscious about his heavily accented English.

"Good cut, Miguel! If you can hit the ball with that power, you'll be sending them out of the park."

When Glen's turn finally came, he stepped into the batter's box, full of confidence. He knocked the mud off his cleats with the bat and turned to face the coach. Glen let the first couple of pitches slide by, waiting for the right one.

"Glen," Coach Johnson said. "What are you waiting for? If I can't see you swing, how can I tell if you can hit the ball? Remember, this is only a practice. I want to see your stance and if you can keep your eye on the ball. Just swing at the pitches I throw. Step into them if you have to."

Glen gritted his teeth and waited for the next pitch. He wasn't going to swing at lousy pitches, no matter what the coach said. How could he prove how well he could hit if all the pitches were out of the strike zone? Remembering everything that he and Jacob had practised, he swung the bat at the next good pitch and connected at the sweet spot.

"Wow!" Ravi exclaimed. "What a hit, Glen."

"Yes, Glen," the coach agreed. "That's what I want to see. We can really build on that kind of thing."

Glen's turn at the plate had made him feel even more confident. All the hard work at the batting cages over the winter had been well worth it. Glen stepped out of the batter's box, removed his helmet, and ran his fingers through his blond hair. He glanced over at the tennis courts and saw that four girls from school had finished their game and were watching the practice. They smiled as Glen looked over, and he smiled back. He didn't know Emiko or Sarah very well, but he knew Colleen, Ryan's sister, and her best friend, Maria.

Glen was conscious of the girls watching them as the boys spread out on the diamond, running a drill. The coach explained the basics; the object was to work as quickly as possible, keeping the throws accurate.

"I will hit the balls out. If you field a ball, throw it to third base. The third baseman will throw it to first. From first base, it goes to second, then to the back catcher at home. Be sure to be in position," the coach explained. "Then, the boy who fielded the ball goes to first base, first goes to catcher, catcher to third, third to second, and so on. Ready?"

Glen soon forgot everything else and concentrated on fielding the ball, throwing it quickly, and getting into position. Several boys had trouble remembering which position to take, and many balls were overthrown in the excitement.

The coach kept things moving at a good pace, encouraging the boys to help each other and call the plays. Glen only slipped up once, when he noticed that the girls were sitting on the hill. Maria seemed to be watching only him.

"That's okay, Glen," Coach Johnson said. "That's the first time you let your concentration go. I'm really pleased with what you're doing."

Giving the boys a few minutes to catch their breath and get something to drink, the coach announced that they would each have a chance to try pitching if they wanted.

"Glen," Jacob said, coming over to his friend. "Are you going to go for it?"

"Sure! I've been playing great today. And I think Maria has noticed too. Don't look!" He grabbed Jacob as he started to turn around.

"Maria, eh?" Jacob grinned. "She's cute."

The coach called the boys back onto the field, telling those who wanted to pitch to grab their gloves and a few balls. Four team members, Glen, Michael, Ryan, and Chris all stepped forward.

The rest of the team took turns hitting the pitches while the coach watched the four boys intently. Glen had been right about Michael; his pitching was as good as ever. He was surprised at how well Ryan pitched, but he was quite sure that he was better than Chris.

After fifteen minutes, the coach halted the practice. "Okay, boys, that's it. If you can all come over to the bench, I'll assign the positions."

Glen's stomach was doing flip-flops. He wanted so much to be a pitcher, to be able to tell his dad that he had succeeded.

"Steve and Maurice, you two are the utility players," the coach began. "That means I can call on you to play any of the positions, but you won't start most games."

Maurice looked down and scuffed the ground with the toe of his cleats.

"Don't look so disappointed, Maurice," the coach said. "You'll get lots of playing time, and you'll gain a lot of experience. Every member of the team has an important part to play."

"The back catcher will be Miguel," Coach Johnson went on. "First base is Jacob, second is Ravi, third is Kamal, and the shortstop will be Marco."

"Way to go, Jacob," Glen slapped his friend on the back. "First base sees a lot of action."

He was holding his breath as the coach continued down the list. There were only a few positions left to assign.

"In right field, we have Nick. In centre field, we have the energetic Ken." The coach paused, rereading the list to himself. Glen thought he was going to explode. "Left field goes to Chris."

"Yes!" Glen yelled without thinking, and the team laughed.

"Our pitchers, obviously, include Glen, Ryan, and Michael," the coach smiled. "It was a great first practice, and I think we have a good team this year. I'm looking forward to working with each of you. We will be playing Tuesday and Thursday evenings, and your families are welcome to come. The games are only six innings long, so expect to be here for about an hour. We play the same team twice in a week, but little league rules say that a pitcher can't pitch more than six innings a week."

Glen was disappointed with that news. He had wanted to be the main pitcher, with the other two as backup.

"We'll be playing the Brampton Bears next week and the Pickering Pythons the week after that," Coach Johnson said. "Make sure you arrive at the diamond half an hour early to warm up." He looked meaningfully at Ryan.

Talking excitedly about their positions on the team, Jacob and Glen didn't notice that Andrew was standing beside the bikes.

"Glen," Andrew said. "I was just on my way home and saw you guys finishing up. Want to put your bikes in the truck and I'll drive you home?"

"Sure, Mr. White," Jacob replied, before Glen could refuse. "I know I'm tired after that workout!"

Glen glared at Jacob. He had wanted to ride home and talk more about the team. He didn't want to do that with Andrew there. He trudged up the hill sullenly.

Climbing into the truck, Jacob kept chattering about the team, but Glen wasn't in the mood to talk about it now.

"So, how'd it go, guys?" Andrew asked, turning up Broadview Avenue.

"Amazing," Jacob replied. "I can't believe that I'm playing first base. Some of the other guys were really good."

"What about you, Glen?" Andrew enquired. "Did you make pitcher?"

"Yeah, I did," was Glen's short reply.

"You should see Glen on the mound," Jacob went on. "He's easily the best pitcher we've got."

"Don't worry, I'll see him play," Andrew said. "We're looking forward to coming to the games." He smiled at the boys, but Glen was looking out the window, paying no attention to the conversation. Glen felt as if Andrew were intruding. He had wanted to rehash the practice with Jacob, but felt like he shouldn't discuss the other players in front of Andrew. Andrew always told him not to say things about people behind their backs that he wouldn't say to their faces.

Jacob filled the silence, telling Andrew how well the practice had gone and who was on the team. Jacob asked Glen if he could stop at Glen's house and borrow a video game.

Getting out of the truck, Andrew tried again to pull Glen into the conversation. "Who are you playing next week, Glen? Are you going to start?"

"Some team from the west end, I think," Glen mumbled. "Don't know if I'm starting. Listen, I'm going to take Jasper and walk Jacob home, okay?"

Andrew took the boys' bikes out of the back of the truck. "Sure," he sighed. "But be home when the streetlights come on."

Glen quickly ran in the house to grab the game and Jasper's leash and rushed back outside. "Come on, Jasper. Let's go for a walk!" he called. The dog came bounding after him.

Walking his bike, Jacob asked Glen why he was so angry at Andrew. "He seems like an okay guy," Jacob said.

"He's not bad, but now that he's married to my mother, there is no chance my parents can get back together," Glen said grudgingly. "I guess that I had always hoped that they might. And if that wasn't bad enough, Megan lives with us now, too."

"What's so bad about Megan? I would love to have a little sister." Jacob was an only child.

"But she takes up all my mom's attention now," Glen complained. "Just because she's a girl and likes to do all that *girl* stuff. My mom hardly seems to have any time for me anymore."

"Go easy on Megan," Jacob said. "She's still a little kid. You told me Megan was only a year old when her mom died."

"I know," Glen reluctantly agreed. "But we were fine before Andrew came along, and now everything's different. He's nothing like my dad and I don't know why my mother married him. My dad drives a sports car and Andrew drives an old truck. My dad makes lots of money and Andrew doesn't —"

"But, Glen," Jacob interrupted gently. "You haven't seen your dad since he moved to California. Andrew's here every day."

"So what!" Glen turned on his friend angrily. "That doesn't matter. I talk to him all the time and he sends me stuff. Andrew can never take his place!"

"Why can't you like them both?"

Just then, the streetlights came on, giving Glen a good excuse to finish the conversation.

"I've got to go," Glen said, pulling Jasper in the opposite direction. "I'll see you later."

Glen stalked off, not waiting for Jacob to reply. Glen couldn't believe that his best friend didn't understand. Sure, Andrew was okay, but that wasn't the point. As far as Glen was concerned, his real dad should come first in his life. Whenever he found himself starting to like Andrew, he felt a little guilty.

"Come on, Jasper," he sighed. "Let's go home."

3

Just Trying to Help

I hope everyone is on their toes tonight," Glen said to Jacob as they locked their bikes and walked towards the bench.

"Lay off the guys, Glen. Everyone is getting a little tired of hearing what you have to say. I heard them telling the coach they're not having any fun."

"If they can't take the heat ..." Glen left the sentence unfinished.

The Eagles had been playing together for about two and a half weeks, and were now one of the top three teams in their division. Tonight, they were playing their second game this week against the Mississauga Panthers. Glen hoped that everyone remembered who the hitters were on the opposing team. He really wanted to beat the Panthers — they were the defending champions from last year.

Jacob waved to the rest of the team. "Just try to keep your thoughts to yourself, okay?"

The Panthers had beaten the Eagles on Tuesday, and Glen was determined that it wouldn't happen again, no matter what.

Dropping his bag on the bench, Glen called the team together for a meeting. "I want everyone to play better than they did last game," he began.

His teammates exchanged glances. "Who died and made you team manager?" Chris glared angrily at Glen, his eyes magnified by the lenses of his glasses.

"Well, someone has to try and take the lead here. Why shouldn't it be me? I make the fewest errors of anyone."

A few boys groaned and turned away from Glen. "Forget it, Glen." Chris picked up a bat to take a few practice swings. "You're hardly the right guy to be giving a pep talk to us!"

Glen looked at Jacob and shook his head. "You just can't talk to some people."

The Eagles were visitors this time and batted first. Coach Johnson always changed the batting order to allow each player a chance to bat leadoff. This time, Miguel was first up, and Glen sat with his arms folded, ready to identify any problems the other guys were having at the plate.

Miguel hit a solid single to the gap in left and was safe at first. Marco came up next. Glen remembered that he hadn't been keeping his eye on the ball lately.

"Don't swing at garbage!" Glen called. "I'll tell you when to swing. Make the pitcher throw to you."

"Ball four!" the umpire called, and the Eagles had two men on base with none out.

"See! I told you!" Glen had planted himself firmly behind the screen where the batters couldn't miss seeing him. "Just listen to me and we'll do fine."

Just like Marco, Ken was too ready to swing, Glen thought. Ken was kind of hyper and couldn't seem to wait at the plate at all. He swung at the first pitch, and Glen winced, closing his eyes. Hearing the bat connect, his eyes flew open again. Ken had hit it just over the infield, but the centre fielder was playing shallow.

Scooping up the ball on the run, the fielder glanced at third. Miguel had been running hard and Glen knew that there was little chance that the fielder could get the ball to third in time. He was right, and the fielder fired to second, nailing Marco on the force. Ken was just touching first, so there was no chance of a double play.

Glen shook his head. "Ken! Why didn't you wait on the pitch? We could have loaded the bases, or better yet, scored a run." Glen saw Coach Johnson glance at him, but the coach didn't say anything.

Glen was on the bench and Ryan would be pitching the first part of the game. Stepping into the batter's box, Ryan ran his hand through his red hair and then smiled disarmingly at the pitcher. Glen almost laughed. Ryan had his own way of throwing off the other team's concentration. Glen knew the Panthers' pitcher was uncertain whether Ryan's smile meant he was a good hitter, and he kept the ball away from the heart of the plate. Glen knew that was what Ryan had wanted, as he was an outside-pitch hitter.

Glen saw one coming in on the outside corner. Ryan stepped into the pitch and launched it deep to right. The fielder had been playing shallow and raced back to the fence after the ball. Miguel scored easily from third, and Ken was running hard. Coach Johnson waved him on from third, and Ryan, hoping to protect the lead runner, tried to stretch the hit into a double.

"Ryan! What are you doing? Stop! You can't run fast enough to make it!" Glen was jumping up and down behind the screen.

Back at the fence, the fielder threw the ball into the cutoff man, who went for the easier out at second. Ryan slid into the base in a cloud of dust, and as it cleared, Glen heard the umpire call "Safe!"

Despite what Glen had been saying, Ryan had made a good choice. If he had stayed on first, the Panthers would have tried to get Ken out at home. This way, the run scored.

Jacob was up next, and Glen tried to catch his eye. Jacob was a patient hitter and watched two balls come in.

"Don't wait too long, Jacob. You gotta take what you can get from this guy."

Jacob caught a bit of the next pitch, fouling it off. He swung at the next one, meeting the ball cleanly and racing for first, while the spectators cheered.

Ryan had been standing on second, but Glen could see that he wasn't watching Jacob. When Jacob hit the ball, Ryan was slow off the start, stumbling off the base.

"Ryan!" Glen shouted, waving his arms to get the other boy's attention. "Get back! You don't have to run!"

But that slight hesitation had blown Ryan's concentration completely and he ran unthinkingly to third. The Panthers' third baseman already had the ball, and Ryan got caught in a rundown, eventually being tagged out by the second baseman.

Glen hated to see errors like that. As Ryan came off the field, Glen was all over him. "All you had to do was start for third to draw the throw! With no one on first, you didn't have to run and could have stayed on the base. Jacob would have been safe and you would have been too."

"Shut up, Glen!" Ryan turned on him. "If you hadn't been yelling, I wouldn't have stumbled like that."

Kamal was up and seemed a little jittery after Ryan's mistake. Grasping the bat with both hands, he slowly lowered it behind his head, stretching his arms and back. He pulled his baseball cap firmly down over his black, closely cropped curls.

"Don't be so sensitive, Kamal," Glen called. "Think more about yourself and less about what just happened."

The rest of the team were staring at Glen. Even though Kamal was shy, everyone on the team liked him.

Kamal fought back from an oh-and-two count, and watched the third ball come in. Unfortunately, he also let the next pitch go, which was called strike three to end the inning.

"I can't believe this," Glen was muttering as the team took the field. "Hitting is not that hard, and base running doesn't take much brains. We've played these guys before. You guys should know better."

Some players were muttering under their breath, but Glen couldn't make out what they were saying.

Ryan took the mound, and Glen watched his form. He had been surprised at their pitching tryout at how well Ryan pitched. He had a high leg kick that confused the batters about where his release point was.

"Just put that rundown behind you, Ryan. Try to pitch a good inning."

Glen began to lose hope as Ryan walked the first batter and the next two hit singles to load the bases.

"What's wrong with you guys?" Glen was pacing up and down in front of the bench. "You've got to run those balls down. Where's your enthusiasm?" He wished he was out there pitching!

With the second baseman at bat, Glen held his breath. A pitch in the strike zone could mean a grand slam! "Strike one!" the umpire called, and Glen let his breath out in a rush. He hated having to watch from the sidelines — it was too nerve-wracking. "Ball!" The count was one and one and Glen thought he was going to explode. "Strike two!" the umpire called.

"Come on, Ryan," Glen called. "One more. Don't blow it."

"Strike three!" the umpire called, as the batter swung hard at a good pitch. The Eagles cheered and Glen just nodded.

Still with bases loaded, Ryan faced the next batter, the catcher. Despite Ryan's best efforts, the hitter lined one down the left-field side. Chris had been playing a liner and was able to keep the damage to a minimum: one run scored and all runners were safe. With one out, Glen was hoping for a miracle.

The left fielder was up and looked confident to Glen.

"Make sure you know what you're going to do with the ball *before* you get it," he bellowed. He couldn't understand why everyone had such long faces out there.

Ryan wound up and pitched, and Glen could see he wasn't going to play this one safely; he was going right after this guy.

"What are you thinking, Ryan! Pitch around him!"

As Ryan glanced at Glen, the batter swung and shot it straight back at him. He was off-balance and fumbled the ball, dropping it. The runner took off as Ryan struggled to get his hands on the ball. He came up with it and threw to home without hesitating. With the force play on, Miguel held his ground on the plate and the runner was out!

The shortstop popped one up to right field to end the inning. Glen couldn't believe they had gotten out of that one with only one run scoring.

The game went on, with both teams scoring some runs, and making some errors. Glen tried to tell each player what he was doing wrong, hoping to pull out a win after all.

The score in the sixth was seven to four for the Eagles and Glen hoped they could add some insurance runs to protect that lead. He was playing this inning and Glen, Jacob, and Kamal were due up at bat. He chewed his lip nervously. Jacob was a good hitter, but Kamal was an unpredictable player.

Glen let his nerves get the best of him in the final inning, and his at-bat didn't last long. Swinging at the first pitch, he popped it up in the infield. The pitcher moved over, calling the rest of team off and making the first out easily. Jacob didn't fare much better, sending one into the outfield, but right at the centre fielder. Two out. Glen's stomach was tied in knots as he watched Kamal take the plate. The Panthers' pitcher was feeling good, and fired strikes right at Kamal, who couldn't swing the bat fast enough to catch them. "Strike three! Batter's out!" the umpire called.

"Kamal, you've got to practise more!" Glen took the bat from him as he came out of the batter's box. "You swing too slowly all the time."

"I didn't see *you* on base," the other boy responded quietly.

"What?" Glen looked at him incredulously. "If I wasn't pitching now, we'd be losing the whole game. I was just trying to help you, you idiot." He glared at Kamal and grabbed his glove, stalking out to the mound.

The Panthers had the last at-bat, and a chance to win. Glen didn't think he could stand to see his team blow the lead they had. He knew that it all rested with him to get the win; he just couldn't rely on the rest of these guys.

The first hitter struck out and Glen's spirits began to lift. The next batter got on base with a blooper over the infield. The pitcher was up next, and Glen worried about pitchers. They could read the ball better than a lot of other players. He fired in a fast ball, but the pitcher swung and sent it deep to centre.

"Run, Ken! Why the heck were you so shallow?" As far as Glen was concerned, the fielder never knew where to play.

Ken was running hard and caught it at the fence for the out. The runner advanced, but at least they had two out.

With the second baseman up again, Glen could hardly contain himself. They had to make this out. They couldn't afford to let even one run score. He wound up and pitched a strike across the heart of the plate, taking no chances. The hitter fouled off the next pitch for strike two. I've got him, Glen thought. I've just got to keep going after him. He wondered why no one else on the team was giving *him* any encouragement. After all, he held a win or a loss in his hands.

Changing his tactics, Glen threw two balls, but neither one fooled the hitter. On the next pitch, the hitter sent it to second.

The runner stepped off the base, trying to confuse Ravi into throwing to Marco.

"Don't do it, Ravi!" Glen screamed. "Throw to first! Why isn't anyone calling the plays?"

Ravi changed direction in mid throw and threw the ball to first. It was about a foot to the outside. Jacob planted his foot on the base and stretched as far as he could. The ball smacked into his glove just ahead of the runner's foot touching the bag. "Out!" the umpire called. "That's game!"

Glen was pleased that Jacob had made such a great play to end the game. If Jacob had missed the ball, it would have meant extra bases for the runner. If he had come off the bag, the runner would have been safe. Glen glanced over at his team as they were lining up for the handshake and got in line last.

"Good game. Good game. Good game." Glen hated this ritual at the end of a game. The other team had lost, so how had they played a good game? "See you in the championships," he called to the other pitcher, who ignored him.

Glen turned to shake hands with his own team, but they were already packing up and no one said a word to him. Even Jacob just looked at him. Huh, Glen thought to himself, that's gratitude for you.

4

No Shows

Glen and Jacob were warming up for the game against the Oshawa Devils on Tuesday as the ball slammed into Jacob's glove, stinging his palm. "Jeez, Glen," he complained. "Can't you take it down a level? Why are you throwing the ball at me so hard?"

"Sorry, Jacob. I guess I just don't know my own strength."

Jacob smiled tightly at his friend. It seemed to Glen that, since he and Jacob had starting playing ball, Jacob hadn't been as friendly. Glen couldn't understand what Jacob might be angry about. If anyone had a right to be angry, Glen thought, it was him.

"What time is it now?" He scanned the field for his teammates.

"It's about quarter to seven." Jacob looked anxiously at his watch.

"Quarter to seven!" Glen exclaimed. He couldn't believe that only five players on the team had shown up. The games began promptly at seven, and Coach Johnson was adamant about everyone arriving a half-hour early to warm up.

Glen glanced at the coach and saw him pacing nervously beside the bench. He wondered if the rest of the team were skipping the warm-up because they were playing the worst team in the division tonight. He hoped that wasn't the case.

"What's wrong with this team?" Glen chewed his lip, worrying that they might have to forfeit a game. "It's not like these guys don't need all the practice they can get," he muttered to himself.

Jacob stared at his friend in disbelief. "Glen, are you listening to yourself? It's your conceited attitude that is starting to take the fun out of the game. You're always putting someone down, rather than trying to help."

Glen was taken aback at Jacob's words and at the angry tone in his voice. "I'm just telling it like it is," he retorted.

The boys began to halfheartedly toss the ball again, in silence. After speaking to the coach of the Oshawa Devils, the umpire came over to confer with Coach Johnson. Glen, Jacob, Ravi, Steve, Michael, and Kamal looked on anxiously. It was now ten after seven, and the rest of the East York Eagles were nowhere to be seen.

"Boys, can you come over to the bench?" Coach Johnson didn't look happy. "I'm sorry to tell you that we have just forfeited the game. I appreciate that all of you were here on time, but there seems to be a problem on our team." The coach looked at each boy in turn. "Morale seems to be very low, and I'm not entirely sure why. I need you guys to come to me if you're having a problem, or if you can't make it to games. I will be calling the other boys tonight and speaking to them individually." Coach Johnson looked straight at Glen. "Remember, we're a team, and no member of a team is more important than any other. I'll see you at the game on Thursday."

As the boys were packing up, Glen could hardly contain his anger. As soon as the coach left, he exploded.

"I can't believe we would forfeit to the Oshawa Devils!" he yelled. "We could have beaten them blindfolded. How am I ever going to keep my stats up when we're missing games? I can't believe the other guys would do this to me. We even have a winning record so far."

Steve shook his head. "Glen, chill, would ya? We're all ticked off about the game, but you're not making it any better. You're not the only one not playing tonight."

Glen turned on Steve angrily. "That's easy for you to say, Steve; you don't have any stats to worry about. You hardly ever get to play."

"Glen!" Ravi jumped in. "Why are you taking it out on Steve? He was here tonight, too."

"I'm never going to pitch in the championships if this team doesn't get its act together." Glen threw his glove and ball into his baseball bag. "Those guys have been missing practices too, and they really need to practise."

The boys were leaving the field, and Glen and Jacob headed for their bikes.

"It's all about you, isn't it, Glen?" Ravi asked in a parting shot.

Glen pedalled home angrily, not even speaking to Jacob on the way. As they parted at Glen's street, Jacob simply said, "I'll see you at the game on Thursday."

* * *

When Glen and Jacob arrived at the diamond on Thursday night, they were pleased to see that several of their teammates were already there. For once, Glen was happy about playing the same team twice in a week. They would have a shot at the Devils tonight. He was also pleased that his mom would be attending this game; Glen was hoping that he'd have a chance to make the hit-and-run play he was becoming known for. He had been disappointed when his mom had missed the last few games because of work.

The coach called the team over to the bench. "Well, guys, it looks like we have just enough players to go ahead with the game. The only trouble is, Glen, you will have to pitch the entire game. Can you handle that?"

Glen was secretly thrilled at the chance to be the only pitcher, even if it was only against the Devils. "No problem," he replied, trying to keep the excitement out of his voice. "I can do it."

Since the East York Eagles were the home team, they took the field first. As Glen took the mound, he glanced over at the spectators. He saw Joshua and Andrew right away, but couldn't see his mother anywhere. He supposed that she was just running late.

The centre fielder was batting leadoff for the Devils. Glen sized him up, confident that this was an easy out. The batter waited nervously for Glen to throw. Glen wound up and fired a fast ball across the plate. The batter never even swung. "Strike one!" the umpire called.

Glen's next pitch was just outside and the count was one and one. The batter breathed a sigh of relief and shifted anxiously. He swung at Glen's next pitch, but was way out in front of the ball. "Strike two!" the umpire called.

Catching the ball from Miguel, Glen fired it back immediately to the plate. "Quick return," the umpire called. "Illegal pitch," he pointed to Glen. "Ball two."

As Glen started to protest, Coach Johnson silenced him from the bench. "Come on, Glen. You know how it works. Just pitch the way you always do."

Glen turned back to the batter, determined to get this guy out. He wound up and pitched the ball, just catching the inside corner of the plate. "Strike three! Batter's out," the umpire called.

Glen smiled, pleased with the call. The first baseman sauntered into the batter's box and swung at Glen's first offering. He hit it up the middle and easily beat the throw to first, rattling Glen.

The catcher smiled as he came to the plate. Glen's first pitch was a ball. "Shake it off, Glen," the coach called. "Just get your concentration back. You can do it."

The second pitch was right across the heart of the plate. The catcher connected with a loud crack of the bat. Glen's heart sank. "Mine!" Ken called, racing in from centre field. For once Glen was glad that Ken was always on the move early. The fielder dove in for the ball and came up with it cleanly for the second out. He threw it quickly into second, but not in time to get the runner.

Glen was having trouble finding his rhythm again after that close call, and he walked the shortstop in six pitches. He faced the pitcher from the Devils with a little more confidence; he took special delight in throwing the ball well against other pitchers.

"Strike one!" the umpire called, as the first pitch crossed the plate. Glen smiled. The umpire had a generous strike zone and now he knew where it was. The second pitch was fouled off and with the third pitch, Glen moved the batter off the plate and he swung late. "Strike three! Batter's out," the umpire called. That was music to Glen's ears. They were out of the inning, with no runs scored and two runners left stranded.

Glen was batting third in the lineup. He glanced over to where the spectators had spread themselves on the hill overlooking the diamond. Running over to Joshua, Glen asked where their mother was.

"She's really sorry, Glen," Josh explained. "Megan's Brownie leader got sick and they needed someone to fill in at the last minute."

"She's not coming?" Glen looked at his brother in disbelief. "She promised me!"

"I know, Glen," Josh replied. "But it's only one night. You're playing all summer, and Megan really needed her tonight. At least Andrew and I came to watch. You're doing great."

Glen turned his back on his brother and stomped back to the bench. He picked up the bat and began taking practice swings, slicing the bat through the air. Looking at the field, he saw that Ken was back on the bench, and Jacob was up. His friend had just hit the ball and was racing for second base. "Safe!" the umpire called.

"Nice hit!" Glen called to Jacob. "Good thing that guy never learned to throw!"

Overhearing the comment, the pitcher stared at Glen in surprise. "Watch the lip," the umpire warned.

Glen stepped into the batter's box, ignoring the umpire. He stared defiantly at the pitcher and waited for the throw. It was low and outside for ball one. The second and third pitches followed suit. "Come on!" Glen said to the pitcher. "Give me something I can hit!"

"Ball four!" the umpire called. "Take your base."

Glen threw the bat to the bench and went to first, not happy about the walk. Miguel was at bat, and Glen hoped he'd move them around. Miguel was a good hitter. He swung at the first pitch and sent it just over the third baseman's head. The left fielder was playing shallow and scooped it up. It was a force play at third, and Jacob had no chance. Glen slid into second in time to hear the call: "Out at third!"

Muttering to himself, Glen tensed to run as Marco came to bat. With Miguel behind him on first, he'd have no choice but to run on a hit. After two balls, Marco hit a strong shot to right field. Glen took off for third, running hard. The right fielder misjudged the ball and it went over his head. On the signal from the third-base coach, Glen kept running, rounding third and heading for home. Glen's teammates were on their feet, telling him to run hard. He poured on the speed and slid into home, just under the catcher's glove. "Safe!"

The spectators were on their feet too, cheering at the close play. Glen heard Andrew call: "Way to go, Glen! Good hustle!" Glen dusted himself off and went to the bench.

Miguel was still on second base. Kamal was at bat with two outs and the score 1 to 0. Kamal seemed nervous and kept leaning the bat on his shoulder. He swung at the ball, just catching it on the side. It dribbled back to the pitcher, who fielded it easily and threw Kamal out at first.

"Aw, man!" Glen exclaimed. "What were you thinking, Kamal? You know you can't hit with the bat on your shoulder like that! You killed the inning!"

Kamal looked down. Picking up his glove, he trudged out to third base.

During the second inning, Glen couldn't believe how his team was playing. They weren't scoring any runs and they were making errors. On an error by Ravi, the Devils scored their first run.

Slamming his glove down in frustration, Glen called for a conference on the mound. "Ravi! What was that? Can't you make an accurate throw? We can't let them win on errors, you know."

"Get lost, Glen," Ravi replied. "If you didn't let them get on base to begin with, we would be farther ahead and it wouldn't matter."

"Why don't you just worry about yourself and let the rest of us play?" Miguel chimed in.

Furious with their attitude, Glen concentrated on throwing strikes and throwing them as hard as possible. He got out of the inning without any more runs being scored.

Coach Johnson collared Glen as he came off the mound and pulled him aside. "Glen, I don't like what I'm hearing out there," he said. "It is not your job to discipline the team, and there certainly is no call for the putdowns and taunts, of their team or ours. If I hear much more out of you, I will let someone else finish pitching the game. Now sit down and be quiet."

Glen stomped back to the bench, folded his arms, and watched his team bat. He couldn't believe the coach was laying into him when the rest of the team was playing so badly. If they would just listen to him, he could make them better players. Glen could see that Steve stood too far off the plate and would never have the strength to hit the ball well from there. He knew that Chris was always fooled by a low pitch and that even Jacob was swinging too soon half the time. They did manage to score another run in the second, making it 2 to 1 for the Eagles.

Glen was back on top of his game in the third, determined that no one would find fault with his pitching. The first three batters hit singles, but the Eagles did manage to throw out a runner at second. Glen struck out the right fielder and the third baseman without losing his stride.

Jacob led off in the fourth and took a walk. Picking up a bat, Glen turned to Ravi. "I hope this pitcher will give me something I can hit this time." Ravi just shrugged.

Glen stepped into the batter's box and into his stance. The first pitch was just off the mark and he held back for ball one. As soon as the second pitch was delivered, Glen knew it was his. He swung strongly and made good contact, sending it just over the second baseman's head. He was safe at first, but had forced Jacob out at second.

Watching the coach carefully, Glen hoped he'd see the signal for a hit-and-run play. So far, he had never been thrown out, and he knew it could add to their lead. Miguel was a good hitter, and this was the perfect time to call it, with no one else on base.

With the count at one and two, Coach Johnson signalled for the hit-and-run. As soon as the pitcher wound up, Glen tensed. As the ball left the pitcher's hand, Glen exploded off of first base. Miguel swung, protecting his runner. As he made contact with the ball, Glen was already touching second standing up. Glen had another successful attempt to add to his stats. Seeing that the ball had been well hit, he tore for third as Miguel rounded first. "Safe at second and third!" the umpire called.

Glen could feel the adrenaline flowing and waited impatiently at third for Marco to hit. He almost left too early, as the batter swung and struck out. Glen scrambled back to third in time. Kamal was up next, and Glen hoped he could keep it together this time. Kamal hit to shallow left field, just behind third base. Glen sprinted for home, knowing that it would be close. Instead, the player threw to third on a fielder's choice, getting Miguel, but allowing Glen to score before the play.

Coming back to the bench, Glen spoke loudly enough for the other team to hear. "I wouldn't have thrown to third on that play," he said. "Who knows? They might have gotten me at home for the third out and no runs would have scored." No one on his team answered, and no one congratulated him on the hit-and-run play except Jacob.

Through the next two innings, the Devils were held scoreless, while the Eagles added three more runs. Coach Johnson repeatedly warned Glen about his comments as the level of enthusiasm on the Eagles' bench deteriorated. Glen faced the bottom of the Devils' order in the sixth, and struck out all three boys. He was elated, but his teammates just gathered up their equipment and left without a word.

Joshua and Andrew came over and congratulated Glen on a game well played, but Glen's anger spilled over. "But Mom didn't see how well I did," he complained. "Why did she have to help out Megan's troop anyway? Someone else could have done it."

Before either of them could reply, Glen stalked off and grabbed his bike, leaving them staring after him.

Peddling furiously up Broadview Avenue, Glen heard some-one calling his name. Glancing back, he saw Jacob trying to catch up to him and stopped his bike.

"Hey, man, why'd you take off like that?" Jacob stopped in front of Glen and reached for his water bottle. "I turned around and you were racing up the hill." Jacob gulped down some water and wiped his mouth on the back of his hand.

"I don't want to talk about it right now." Glen pushed off from the curb.

Jacob sighed and fell in behind his friend. It was a silent ride home and Glen was relieved when the two boys parted. Passing Andrew's truck, Glen put his bike away in the garage and quietly let himself into the house. He eased the door shut, hoping that Jasper was in the backyard and wouldn't let everyone know he was home. He crept up the stairs, missing the third one that always creaked, went into his room and closed the door.

Glen leaned his back against the door for a moment. He just didn't want to talk to anyone right now. But as he dropped his baseball bag on the floor, there was a quick knock and Joshua stepped in, uninvited.

"What do you want?" Glen kept his back to his brother, not wanting to hear a lecture.

Joshua settled himself at Glen's desk, idly playing with the baseball figures Glen kept there. "I just wondered why you were so angry about Mom missing one of your games."

Glen turned around and stared at Josh for a minute. "Every time I ask her to do something lately she is either at work or doing something with Megan. She has no time for me anymore." He threw his cleats into the closet and sat down on his bed.

"Glen, you have to remember that Megan doesn't know what it's like to have a mother. And Mom has never had a little girl before. She's just trying to build a relationship with Megan and make her feel comfortable here."

"Well, if she's not with Megan, then she is with Andrew," Glen complained.

"Jeez, they've only been married for a couple of months. What do you expect?"

"I don't like having a stepfather. Everything was fine until Andrew moved in. I just can't like him the way you do. Why have you let him take Dad's place so easily?"

"I haven't, Glen." Joshua sighed and came over to sit beside Glen. "But do you remember what it was like around here when Mom and Dad were still together, and then after he left?"

"Yeah, I do. At least everyone was happy."

"I don't think you really do remember, Glen. You were too young to see what was happening. It wasn't easy at all on Mom, and I had to help out a lot. Even when Dad was here, he was never really here for us. He was always away on business, and now he has cancelled his plans every time he has promised to be here. I like having Andrew around."

"You sound like you don't even love Dad any more," Glen said, looking sadly at his dad's picture on his night table.

"Of course I love him. He's still my dad. But it doesn't mean I can't appreciate Andrew and what he's done for us. I like seeing Mom happy. Just because Andrew is in our lives doesn't mean we have to love Dad any less. We don't need to choose between them, Glen, and you don't have to feel that liking Andrew is being disloyal to Dad."

Glen looked at Joshua, surprised that he seemed to understand the conflict he was feeling.

"Maybe you need to think about it a little more," Joshua said as he left the room and closed the door.

Glen stared at the poster of Delgado on the back of his door, not sure what he was feeling. He was still a little upset with his mother, but what Joshua had said made sense. He knew in his heart that his own dad hadn't always been there for them, but he wasn't really ready to accept Andrew as a stepfather. His mom did seem to be happier since the marriage, but he resented not having her all to himself. He had hoped that being on the baseball team would make him more important than Megan, but that wasn't happening. At least his dad would be arriving in less than two weeks to see him play. Maybe he could talk to him about everything.

5

All Wet

This looks like a good spot," Glen said to Jacob, spreading out his big blue beach towel. The boys had decided to spend the day at the pool in Riverdale Park, up the hill from the baseball diamond. It had rained all weekend and most of Monday, spoiling their plans to go swimming then. Jacob spread his towel out beside Glen's.

"Last one in is a rotten egg!" Jacob called, as he jumped into the shallow end. Glen jumped in after his friend, laughing.

With no game scheduled for that evening, the boys wanted to make the most of it. The day was sunny and clear and Glen hoped that by going swimming and relaxing, some of the tension between him and Jacob would disappear. Next to baseball, swimming was one of Glen's favourite pastimes, and Jacob also loved the water. Their Tuesday game the night before hadn't gone very well. The Eagles had lost to the Scarborough Stallions and Glen had exchanged some heated words with Maurice, who had been playing right field.

The boys dove into the deep end. The pool was too crowded to allow them to race, so they decided to practise some diving. Pulling themselves onto the deck, they lined up for the lower of the two diving boards.

"I dare you to do a somersault off the board," Glen said to Jacob.

"You tell me when the lifeguard isn't watching, and I'll do it," Jacob replied, taking the dare. "I just don't want to get kicked out of the pool."

Jacob climbed the ladder slowly, hoping that the lifeguard would look away. He walked to the end of the board and prepared to jump.

"Go!" Glen yelled.

Jacob jumped out from the board and tucked his knees up to his chin, doing a perfect somersault into the water. He came up laughing, shaking the water from his tightly curled black hair.

"If I see that again," a voice said behind him, "you're out of the pool." The lifeguard was pointing right at Jacob.

Laughing, Glen jumped off the diving board. Climbing up the ladder to the deck, Jacob pushed Glen playfully. "You were supposed to be watching the lifeguard!"

"I was! Honestly, he wasn't looking when I told you to go," Glen protested. "But you should have seen your face!" he teased.

They spent the next hour practising their diving and seeing who could hold their breath the longest. They decided to take a break and stretch out on their towels for a while.

"Ah, that sun feels good," Jacob said, settling onto his towel. Glen pulled out his sunscreen and began slathering it on. "Good thing you brought that," he teased Glen. "You wouldn't want to add any more freckles to that face."

"Oh, funny," Glen replied. "I guess you don't have to worry about getting freckles, do you?" he continued, glancing at Jacob's warm brown skin.

"Nope, I have built-in freckle protection." Glen squirted some sunscreen playfully at Jacob.

"Hey, isn't that Maurice over there?" Glen pointed to the other side of the pool. He waved at the other boy, but Maurice didn't return the gesture.

"What's his problem?" Glen asked, annoyed by Maurice's reaction.

"He's probably still angry about what you said in the game last night," Jacob said. "You were kind of brutal, you know."

"What do you mean? I was just telling him the truth. It's not my fault that he can't catch," Glen replied defensively. "Then again, half the team could use some pointers."

Jacob bit his lip, but let the comment slide. Changing the topic, Jacob asked Glen when his dad was coming.

"He's flying in Tuesday morning, before our game," Glen replied happily. "I can't wait to see him. I don't know if Josh is looking forward to it though."

"What do you mean?" Jacob asked, surprised by Glen's comment.

"Well, me and Josh kind of talked about it last Thursday, after the game," Glen stretched out on his towel. "Josh seems to be closer to Andrew than he ever was to our dad. He keeps trying to tell me that things are better now than when my parents were married, but I find it hard to believe."

"Josh is older, you know," Jacob pointed out. "Maybe he remembers things that you don't — he could be right. I know you were disappointed the last couple of times your dad cancelled on you. Have you even seen him since he moved?"

"No, but he is coming this time for sure." Glen took off his sunglasses and looked at Jacob. "Why are you on Josh's side? I thought you were my friend."

Just as Jacob opened his mouth to reply, someone stopped in front of Glen's towel, blocking out the sun. Looking up, Glen saw Maria, Emiko, Colleen, and Sarah standing on the pool deck.

"Hi, guys," Maria said, looking right at Glen. "Can we sit here, too?"

Jacob rolled his eyes.

"Sure," Glen replied, smiling at the girls.

"I saw you at the game last night, Glen," Maria said shyly, twisting her long auburn hair around her finger. "I thought you played really well."

"Thanks," he replied smugly. "Some of the other guys can't get it together on the field, but the pitcher has to be the best. After all, it *is* the most important position."

"Oh," Maria said. She drew down her eyebrows and seemed slightly taken aback by Glen's words.

"I thought that you were just great too, Jacob," Emiko said, turning away from Glen.

"Thanks. It wasn't one of our best games, but we're a pretty good team," Jacob replied.

"If some of the guys don't start playing better, we won't be a good team for long," Glen said. "I keep trying to tell them what they're doing wrong, but they just won't listen to me."

Sarah and Emily looked at each other with their eyebrows raised, and Maria blushed.

"Don't listen to him," Jacob said, trying to lighten the mood. "He just thinks that he's God's gift to baseball."

"I'm the only one on the team who can make the hit-and-run play, you know," Glen reminded everyone.

Sarah dug Maria in the ribs. Jumping to his feet, Glen grabbed the bottle of sunscreen. "Here, let me show you how I pitch a fast ball." He moved away from the group and faced them. Glen wound up for the pitch and as his hand came forward, the bottle of sunscreen slipped from his grasp. It hit the deck in front of Emily, popping open and spraying her.

"Glen!" she cried, pulling her towel out of the way. "What did you do that for, you jerk?"

"It was an accident," he replied sheepishly. "It slipped."

"Glen, just sit down," Jacob snapped. "You're making a fool of yourself."

"I said it was an accident. You're just jealous because I'm a better player than you are, and the girls come to watch me." Glen could feel his face grow hot as he turned on his friend.

"Jealous?" Jacob cried. "At least the rest of the team doesn't hate me. I spend half my time defending you to everyone else."

"Why do you have to defend me? What am I doing wrong?" Glen asked incredulously.

"Everyone is tired of your attitude. You're the reason we're losing games."

"What? Are you saying I'm not a good player?"

The girls started gathering their belongings as the two boys argued.

"I never said you weren't a good player." Jacob shook his head in frustration. "But your attitude is lousy. No one's having fun any more because they are too worried about you mouthing off. That's why we have trouble getting enough guys out to games and practices." Jacob jumped to his feet, pulling his towel with him. "If things don't change soon, there won't be a team left by the championships. I'm getting tried of dealing with your crap too."

Glen stared open-mouthed as his friend stormed off to the change room. He had never heard Jacob so angry about anything before. As Glen turned back to his towel, the girls were moving to another spot on the deck.

"Where are you going?" he asked.

Maria turned around. "Oh, we're just moving to a sunnier spot, Glen. This one is kind of in the shade now."

Glen sat on his towel and watched the girls join Maurice and his friends. They were all whispering and watching Glen out of the corners of their eyes. Maurice said something to Sarah and all the girls snickered and turned away.

Glen put his sunglasses on and tried to look cool, but his stomach was churning. He couldn't believe the things that

Jacob had said, and especially in front of the girls. They were supposed to be best friends. How could Jacob be so jealous of him? He gathered his towel and things together and walked past the girls to the change room. They all ignored him. Even Maria looked away quickly when he caught her eye. Glen had been looking forward to this summer so much and it wasn't turning out the way he had expected at all.

6

Disappointment

B oy, I really hate washing windows," Glen grumbled to himself as he attacked the third section in the dining room. Ever since his argument with Jacob at the pool last week, Glen had been moping around the house. His mother had finally cornered him to help with some chores that they had been putting off all summer.

"You know, this is great exercise for that pitching arm," his mother teased. "We've got to keep you in shape between games." Catherine was trying to lighten Glen's bad mood.

"If the team keeps going the way it has been, we won't need my arm. I sure am glad that Dad wasn't here to see the last few games. Our playing has really stunk and it's just no fun to lose."

"I know that baseball is important to you, Glen, but remember that you're supposed to enjoy playing the game whether you win or lose." His mother turned to look at Glen. "How is your record overall? I thought you told me that the team did well in the first half of the season."

"Yeah, we did all right in the first part, but now we're on a losing streak. If Dad had seen those games, he would have been really disappointed. I hope that when he gets here next week the rest of the team can get its act together."

Catherine frowned at Glen's remarks. "You know, Andrew thinks that your team plays pretty well together," she said. "Remember that there is no 'I' in 'team,' Glen."

Glen rolled his eyes. He wished that his mother wasn't so fond of those corny clichés.

"How does Jacob feel about the team? You were both really looking forward to playing together, and I haven't seen him around for the last few days."

Glen was silent for a moment. He hadn't told his mother about his argument with Jacob and what had happened at the pool. Although he felt that he was right about the team, he wasn't happy about arguing with Jacob. They had been such good friends for the past three years, and Glen had felt a little lost over the weekend not hanging out with him. But as far as Glen was concerned, he had nothing to apologize for. Just as he was about to answer his mother's question, the phone rang.

Catherine dashed into the kitchen, grabbing the phone on the fourth ring. Glen could only hear part of the conversation, and he didn't really pay any attention until he heard his mother say his dad's name. Glen could tell that his mother was upset about something, and his stomach knotted. Surely his dad was only calling to confirm his arrival time. But Glen knew that wouldn't upset his mother. He heard her say quietly: "No, Bob, you'll have to do it yourself. Wait a minute."

"Glen?" she called. "Your dad is on the phone and needs to talk to you."

Glen put down the rag, and climbed slowly off the chair. With a feeling of dread, he walked into the kitchen and took the phone from his mom. Catherine moved slightly behind Glen, squeezing his shoulder.

"Hi, Glen," his dad said. "I've got some bad news for you, but I know you'll understand. The meetings in Toronto have been moved to Seattle, and —"

"You're not coming, are you?" Glen cut his dad off abruptly.

"No, Glen, I can't make it up there this summer."

"Why not, Dad? You promised you'd be here this time."

"You have to understand, Glen. I have no choice. I have to attend the meetings, and I can't help the fact that the company switched locations. Maybe we can get together in the fall."

"But I told my friends that you were coming and you promised that you'd watch me pitch."

"I know, Glen, but what do you want me to do?"

"I want you to keep your promise!"

"For goodness sake, Glen, it's only a baseball game I'm missing. I'll be there in the fall."

Glen was fighting back the tears. He felt sick to his stomach with disappointment. How could his dad not understand how important it was to Glen to see him and show him how well he played? Baseball was something that Glen was really good at, and he wanted his father to be proud of him. He couldn't believe that Josh was right and that his dad was bailing on him again.

"Yeah, whatever, Dad. Look, I have to go now." He angrily brushed the back of his hand across his eyes. Without waiting for a reply, he hung up the phone.

Turning around, Glen was surprised to see his mother and Andrew standing in front of him. He hadn't heard Andrew come in, but knew from the concerned looks on their faces that they had heard the whole conversation. He was angry with his father, but he didn't want Andrew or his mom to see him crying.

"I'm sorry, Glen," she said quietly. "I know he's not coming and that he let you down again."

Glen could tell that his mother hadn't been surprised about the cancellation of his dad's trip. She seemed to expect the worst from him.

"Since I'm home early, do you want me to come to your game tonight?" Andrew tried to put an arm around Glen's shoulders.

"Why would I want you to come to my game?" Glen exploded, throwing Andrew's arm off. "You're probably the reason that my dad isn't coming!" Glen knew he wasn't making any sense and that Andrew had nothing to do with it, but he wanted to hurt someone as badly as he was hurting now. "You're just a pretend father anyway!"

"Glen, that's enough!" his mother warned. "I know you're upset and angry, but you can't take it out on other people. Andrew was just trying to help."

"I don't need his help!" Glen was crying now. "If Andrew wasn't here, Dad would have tried harder to get here, I know he would have."

"Glen, you're not making any sense now. This has nothing to do with Andrew. It was your father who cancelled his trip." Catherine tried to gather her son into her arms.

"Don't touch me!" Glen pulled away from his mother and grabbed his baseball bag from the kitchen chair. "I don't need anyone!" He ran out of the kitchen and down the hall to the front door. Tearing it open, Glen flew down the front steps, ignoring his mother's calls for him to come back. Grabbing his bike from the garage, he pedalled as hard as he could down Beechwood, trying to leave his anger behind.

Without thinking, Glen almost made the turn to go meet Jacob. They had always ridden to the games together, and he wished more than ever that he and Jacob had not argued at the pool last week.

Riding alone down Broadview, Glen thought about his dad and again had to fight back the tears. He hated to admit, even to himself, that Josh might have been right. Maybe business *was* more important to his dad than his family was. He *had* been young when his father was still at home, and maybe he didn't remember everything clearly. Glen was beginning to feel a bit bad about what he had said to Andrew before he had left the house. He had been so hurt and upset with his dad that he had lashed out without thinking. Now he was beginning to feel foolish that he had trusted his dad to keep his word, and he was angry at him for making him feel this way. It had been difficult enough for Glen to cope with the breakup of his family, his dad's moving so far away, and his mother's second marriage. His dad could make it so much easier if he could just keep his promises. Now Glen knew that he couldn't rely on him for anything.

As Glen neared Riverdale Park, he was angrier than ever. By the time he had chained up his bike and had begun warming up, he was in a thoroughly foul mood. The Eagles were playing the Woodbridge Cougars tonight, and they were a good team. Glen just hoped that he wouldn't have to carry his teammates. He was in no mood to cope with guys who couldn't play ball.

The only bright spot came when Coach Johnson announced that Glen would be starting the game. Glen was pleased that he was the starting pitcher, but he couldn't seem to shake his anger, even with that good news. The Eagles were visitors this game; they would bat first.

Kamal led off. As Kamal took his place in the batter's box, Glen couldn't help thinking that he never looked ready to swing. It deceived the other pitchers, and this time was no different. Kamal hit an easy ball to right field and was safe at first. Ravi managed to move Kamal to second, and Marco was up third. Glen hoped that Marco wouldn't swing at the first pitch the way he usually did.

"Ball one!" called the umpire. The Cougars' pitcher wound up and delivered a heater across the plate. Marco connected, sending a liner screaming down the left-field line. It smacked straight into the third baseman's glove, and Kamal and Ravi scrambled back to their bases.

Glen glanced at Jacob as his friend walked to the plate. He wanted to say something to him, but just couldn't bring himself to do it. Glen concentrated on watching the pitcher and judging the pitches he threw. He saw that the first two strikes barely caught the outside corner of the plate and hoped that the umpire was that generous with his strike zone when he was pitching. At a count of two and two, Jacob sent one up the middle. Ravi and Kamal poured on the speed. "Safe at third and home!" the umpire yelled. With Jacob on first and Ravi on third, Glen just hoped that he could come through for the team now. Stepping up to the plate, he stared hard at the pitcher, hoping to throw him off balance.

"Strike one!" Glen gritted his teeth.

"Ball one!"

The pitcher's next offering was just the kind of pitch Glen liked and he swung through, sending the ball just over the first baseman's head into right field. He raced for first and heard the "Safe!" call just before the ball came into the base.

Standing at first, Glen kept an eye out for the hit-and-run sign, hoping the coach would send him. Nick was up to bat, and he wasn't their strongest hitter. Glen knew that if the coach called the hit-and-run play, he could then make it home on a single from second. He needed to be in scoring position. Glen's heart sank as he watched Nick catch a piece of a pitch that was clearly a ball. It bounced back to the pitcher, who dove on it and threw to second. It was a force play and Glen was out. He tried to block the throw to first, but the second baseman was too quick. The Cougars turned a double play and the first half of the inning was over.

Jogging in to get his glove, Glen stared darkly at Nick. He barely managed to keep his mouth shut and his mood continued to worsen.

Taking the mound, Glen fired some warm-up pitches at Miguel. The shortstop for the Cougars was first up and Glen threw all his feelings into his pitches, striking the other boy out on five pitches.

So far, so good, Glen thought. He watched the pitcher walk confidently to the plate. As the ball left Glen's fingers, he knew he had given him the perfect hitter's pitch. It had no curve at all and was right over the heart of the plate. Cursing silently, Glen saw the other player hit it into the gap. Only Nick's quick reaction in right field kept it to a single.

The first baseman was a strong-looking boy and Glen pitched to him carefully. He was pleased to see that the umpire had kept the same generous strike zone for Glen as he had had for the Cougars' pitcher. With a count of two and one, the hitter got all of the pitch, sending it to left field. It bounced just in front of Maurice, who had been playing too deep, and the runner stretched it out to a double, moving the lead runner to third. Yanking his glove off, Glen slammed it down and stared out at Maurice.

Pointing at Glen, the umpire barked, "I don't want to see any more outbursts from you!"

Sullenly, Glen picked up his glove and dusted it off. Facing the left fielder, Glen couldn't seem to find the plate again, and walked him to load the bases. How was he going to get out of this one with no earned runs? He took a deep breath, trying to calm down and deliver. The centre fielder swung at the first pitch, sending it almost straight back to Glen. Still moving from delivery, Glen was off balance and had no chance to grab the ball. Glen's body blocked the play from Ravi, who went left instead of right and had no time to recover. The pitcher scored easily, and the runners were all safe.

Glen was glad that he had gotten the first batter out, or they'd really be in trouble. The second baseman was a good runner, and Glen hoped to get him out on strikes rather than chance him on the bases. The umpire called strikes one and two. The hitter watched Glen's third pitch all the way, and even Glen had to admire his nerve. He connected on Glen's next pitch, sending the ball just over the shortstop's head.

Maurice ran in and scooped it up, looking around the bases wildly, unsure of where to throw. Another run scored and the centre fielder was gunning for home. Maurice hesitated and the second baseman tried for second to draw the throw and protect the runner. Maurice took the bait, throwing to second and getting the out, but letting the runner score. The Cougars were up 2 to 3 with a man on third.

"Maurice!" Glen called. "How could you fall for that? Always go for the runner! He wanted you to throw to second. Jeez!"

Glen turned back to face the next batter, the third baseman. He threw the pitches hard and fast across the plate. When the hitter finally caught one, it came straight back at Glen. This time, he was ready and snagged the liner for the out. But it had been a costly inning.

Coming off the mound, Glen was muttering, just loudly enough for the team to hear, about errors and knowing what play to make before the ball came to you. The rest of the team ignored him.

Miguel led off the inning with a single and Ken followed with another. Maurice had been struggling at the plate lately and was batting last in the lineup. Swinging at what Glen thought was obviously a ball, Maurice popped it up. "Infield fly — batter's out!" the umpire called. Glen threw his glove down in frustration and rolled his eyes as Maurice sat down again.

Kamal kept the bat off his shoulder and loaded the bases for Ravi. Glen crossed his fingers for a hit, and Ravi came through, hitting a solid liner that blew past the shortstop and scored Miguel. Ken had no choice but to take off for third and was thrown out on the force. Marco stepped up to bat and Glen could see that he meant to do some damage. He waited for his pitch and swung, arms fully extended. As soon as he heard the crack, Glen knew it was gone. Marco had hit a homer and scored three runs, giving them back the lead! Everyone lined up on the third-base line to high-five Marco as he came in.

Jacob stepped up to the plate and Glen waited in the on-deck position outside the fence. He wanted to bat this inning, and get the hit-and-run play. Maybe he'd even try for a home run. He watched Jacob take two pitches without swinging and tensed. The third pitch was a good one, and Jacob was way behind the pitch. "Strike three! Batter's out!" the umpire called.

Every time they had a rally going, Glen thought, someone got overanxious or screwed it up. Throwing the bat down, he picked up his glove and ran out to the mound. It looked as if he would have to carry the team after all.

The catcher led off the home half of the third inning. He liked to chase pitches, and Glen was more than happy to oblige, striking him out in four. Back at the top of the order, the shortstop hit one up the middle for the first single. Glen shook his head. The pitcher was next. Glen took his time, making sure the delivery was perfect and his aim was true. "Strike one!" called the umpire. Glen stayed focused on the hitter and gave him nothing to hit until the count was full. Not wanting to strike out, the other boy swung, popping it up to Ken in shallow centre field for an out. The runner never moved off first.

Glen pitched well to the next two batters, but they both hit singles, loading the bases for the centre fielder. A single here would score a run! Glen pitched quickly, but not so fast as to be called on a quick return — he didn't want to walk in a run.

"Ball!" called the umpire on Glen's first offering. "Ball two!" He had let the batter get ahead in the count now and had to go after him. "Strike one!" That was better. The batter swung at the next pitch, sending it just past the infield and scoring a run.

Frustrated, Glen sized up the second baseman, knowing that he'd been out at second last time.

"Make sure you know where you're going to throw before you get the ball!" he called to his teammates.

Knowing that he couldn't be called on a balk in little league, Glen motioned to pitch and stepped off the rubber. The runners had been tensed to run and moved off their bases. Quickly, Glen fired to first. "Out at first!" the umpire called. Those were the sweetest words Glen had heard all day. He had picked off the runner at first to end the inning.

Glen ran off the mound, eager to bat. He hit a solid single and waited on first for a sign from the coach. They needed a runner in scoring position now, but Coach Johnson wasn't giving Glen the signal. Not waiting for it, Glen took off as soon as the ball left the pitcher's hand. Nick, seeing Glen running on the oh-and-two count, swung to protect Glen and struck out. Glen came in safe at second, but he could see that the coach was pacing up and down at the bench. Sure, he hadn't had the signal, but he was safe! Glen was watching the coach and was slow off the mark when Miguel hit the ball. He still thought he could beat the throw to third and ran. Coming in, Glen was sure he was there before the throw, but the umpire called him out. Ken's at-bat was short as he fouled out on three pitches.

Coach Johnson had had enough. "Glen, you're sitting now and Michael is in. Steve, you go out to left field for Maurice and we'll try to shake this game up a little. Glen, come here, please."

Glen walked slowly over to where the coach was standing. "Don't ever take the initiative to run a play I haven't called," the coach said. "We scored no runs in that inning because of it. You have an awful lot to say to the rest of the team when something goes wrong. I don't want you undermining them. Now sit down and keep your lip zipped."

Glen's face reddened with anger. I can't believe the coach would talk to me like that, he thought. Well, now that I'm sitting, let's just see how well they do. I am the only thing holding this team together!

Michael pitched well through the next four at-bats, and the team seemed to rally once again. The Eagles tied it up in the sixth inning, but the Cougars had the final at-bat. Michael kept his cool and pitched well, giving up only a few hits. With a runner on third and two outs, Glen could hardly stand to be on the bench. His stomach was knotted, watching Michael's delivery for flaws. He was facing the first baseman for the final out, and Michael delivered what even Glen had to admit was a good pitch. The batter waited for it to come to him and stepped into the ball. He hit it hard, but it went high towards left field.

Glen shot to his feet, watching the ball arc out towards the field. It was headed right to Steve and should have been an easy out. Glen watched the younger boy trying to track the ball, running in desperately. Glen could see that Steve was too far infield to make the catch and began yelling instructions.

"Steve! You're too far infield! Can't you see the ball? No! Get back! Are you blind?" Steve glanced at the bench in confusion, trying to figure out where he should stop. Taking his eye off the ball for that split second broke his concentration and the ball landed just past him. The runners on base took off as soon as the ball touched green, and Ken came tearing in from centre to make the play. By that time, it was too late. The Cougars' lead runner had already crossed home plate and the game was over. The Eagles had lost.

7

Going Too Far

As the opposing team ran out on the field and congratulated each other, Glen tore onto the field, making a beeline for Steve. Standing right in front of the younger boy and towering over him, Glen lost it.

"How could you be so stupid!" he yelled. "All you had to do was move back a little and it would have been in your glove."

"I'm sorry, Glen. I couldn't see the ball and I got confused with you yelling from the bench," Steve said timidly. His face was drained of colour and he was blinking nervously.

"I don't even know why you're on this team!" Glen was waving his arms around wildly. "We would have won if you hadn't been out there."

The rest of the team had stopped what they were doing and were watching the exchange. Jacob took one look at Glen's face, dropped his baseball bag, and ran over to the two boys.

"Glen! Calm down. It's not worth getting so worked up about. Everyone makes errors." Jacob reached out and put a hand on Glen's shoulder.

Glen spun around. "Stay out of this, Jacob. It's got nothing to do with you."

"Of course it does! I'm on this team too. You're acting like a spoiled brat!" Jacob tried to move past Glen to speak to Steve.

Reacting without even thinking, Glen put his two hands on Jacob's chest and shoved him back hard. Surprised, Jacob was knocked to the ground and stared up at Glen in disbelief. The whole team had gathered around by now, and they all fell silent. Glen was horrified at what he had just done. Jacob was his best friend! He stared at Jacob, unable to say anything to him.

Jacob picked himself up and dusted his pants off. "You are the biggest jerk I have ever met!" Jacob starting moving towards Glen with his fists clenched. "I am the only guy on this team who'll still talk to you, and this is how you treat me?"

Just then, Coach Johnson burst into the circle. He sized up the situation and put a restraining hand on Jacob's arm. "All right you guys, that's enough. I won't tolerate any fighting on this team. The rest of you, pack up your stuff and go home. Glen, I want to talk to you privately."

Jacob never looked back as he walked away from Glen. Glen stared at his friend's back, feeling sick about what he had just done. How did things get so out of control? He had never meant to hurt Jacob and would give anything to go back and change it. All his anger had left him. Walking over to the bench with the coach, Glen braced himself for the worst.

"Glen," Coach Johnson began. "I'm so disappointed in you. I don't know what's gotten into you lately, but it's obvious that something has. This behaviour can't continue. I really should release you from the team, but I'm going to give you one more chance. I'm going to bench you for the next game. You are welcome to come and watch, but I don't want to hear a peep out of you or you're finished for the season."

Glen hung his head, relieved that he was still on the team. But the Eagles had to win the next game to go the championships. How could they win, if he didn't pitch? At least he would be able to play the championship if they did win. Glen was reeling from everything that had just happened and feeling sick about pushing Jacob. He couldn't believe how everything was turning out.

As the coach walked away from Glen, he looked up to see Joshua standing by the running track with Jasper. Glen wondered how much Josh had heard. His brother waved and walked over to where he was standing. Glen tried to look as though nothing had happened.

"Hey, Glen, did you guys win?" Josh asked casually.

"No, we didn't," Glen replied, looking at the ground. "It fell apart in the last inning." He could feel Josh's eyes on him and he tried to keep his face neutral.

"Why don't you walk your bike and we'll go home together?" Josh asked.

Glen had a sneaking suspicion that Josh had walked Jasper to the baseball diamond on purpose. His mom and Andrew had probably filled Josh in on the argument they had had before the game. Glen shrugged his shoulders, grabbed his baseball bag, and went to unlock his bike.

Taking a deep breath, Glen asked, "I guess you heard that Dad's not coming this summer, right?"

"Yeah, Mom told me. I was disappointed, but I can't say that I was really surprised. You should have known that this would happen, Glen. I know it's not easy, but that's just the way Dad is, and you need to learn to accept these things."

The two brothers walked past Loblaws in silence, each thinking about their dad.

"Did Mom tell you what happened after Dad called too?" Glen asked, not looking at Josh.

"Yeah, she told me that you were pretty angry and took it out on Andrew. That wasn't really fair," Josh told him.

"If Mom hadn't married Andrew, I wouldn't be having such a crappy summer."

"Glen, you've got to stop blaming other people for your problems! Why don't you try asking Andrew to come to a game? He'd be more than happy to do it. He's really trying to be a friend to you."

Glen bit his lip. "I sort of realize that now," he said reluctantly. "I guess I wanted to believe that Andrew was the problem, not Dad. But now I can't ask Andrew to come to a game." Glen paused.

"Why not?" His brother was looking right at him, and there was no point trying to lie.

"Well, I kind of got in trouble after the game. Coach benched me for the next one."

"I thought that you looked pretty upset when I saw you talking to the coach. Want to tell me what happened?"

"You have to promise not to tell Mom, okay?" Glen asked.

"Fine, I won't tell," Josh agreed reluctantly.

"Well, I was really angry after Dad's phone call and the argument, and I lost my temper with the guy who dropped the ball and made us lose the game. Then, Jacob came up to us, I guess to try and smooth it over, and I'm not sure how it happened, but I shoved him to the ground."

"What!" Josh exclaimed. "Was he hurt?"

"No, he was okay, but he was so angry at me. We also argued last week at the pool and weren't really talking yet. Now I'm not sure if we'll ever be friends again."

"I can't believe it, Glen. You're really out of control, you know. You need to step back and think before you do things. Maybe this benching will be a good time for that. You know, until you sort this out with Andrew, nothing else is going to get any better."

Glen heaved a long sigh. Josh might be right, but Glen was in no mood for good advice.

The boys had turned into their driveway and Glen put his bike away in the garage. He noticed that Andrew's truck wasn't in the driveway, and wondered where he had gone. He couldn't help feeling a little relieved.

Glen headed straight for the kitchen and made himself a sandwich. His mother was in the living room, and hadn't said anything to him when he came in. He took his food and his baseball bag up to his room, hoping that maybe he wouldn't have to talk to anyone until tomorrow.

Glen wolfed down the sandwich and hopped into the shower. The warm water was soothing after his hard day, and he began to feel really tired. He towelled off and got right into his pyjamas, whistling for Jasper. The big dog came bounding into the bedroom and leapt up on Glen's bed.

A few minutes later, Catherine also came into Glen's room. "I heard you whistle for Jasper and thought that you might be calling it a day a little earlier than usual," his mother said. "I want to talk to you before you go to sleep."

Crossing the room, Catherine sat on the other side of the bed. "Andrew and I agreed that I would talk to you by myself about what happened today," she began.

Glen stared down at the bedspread, petting Jasper slowly.

"I know that you're really disappointed about your dad not coming this summer," she went on. "It must be very difficult when someone breaks their promises to you so often, especially a parent. I know that your dad does love you and Josh, but his work has always ruled his life. That was one of the reasons why he and I divorced, Glen."

Glen glanced at his mother, reassured by the calm tone of her voice.

"Andrew has never tried to take your dad's place, but he could be a good friend to you, if you would just let him. Andrew is a nice guy, and so is your father, but they are very different from each other. You can appreciate the good qualities they each have without feeling guilty, you know."

"I feel bad about what I said to Andrew," Glen said quietly.

"I think that you should tell him that at breakfast tomorrow. He'd really appreciate it. And I want you to promise me that you'll give Andrew a chance to be your friend."

"I guess I can," Glen mumbled. He debated about telling his mother what had happened at the game that day. He really wanted to come clean about everything and just maybe salvage some of this summer. He hoped that his mother would be sympathetic to him. As Catherine reached over and hugged Glen, he confessed that he had been benched after yelling at Steve and pushing Jacob.

Catherine sat back, surprised. "Glen, this is really serious."

He nodded silently.

"No matter how angry you get, you should never resort to violence to solve your problems. I'm surprised that your coach agreed to let you stay on the team, and I think the benching is a fair punishment. You also owe Jacob and Steve and the team an apology."

Glen was crestfallen at his mother's reaction. He had hoped that she would side with him — at least a little.

"Rather than grounding you, I want you to go to the game anyway. I think it would be good for you to sit on the sidelines. I'm going to call Coach Johnson in the morning."

Shocked, Glen couldn't believe that his mom would make him go to the game. He had hoped that he wouldn't have to face the team until it had all blown over. What if no one talked to him?

"Do I make myself clear, Glen?" his mother finished.

"Yes," he muttered, looking down. There was no point in arguing.

"Okay. Now settle down and get a good night's sleep," Catherine said, leaning over and kissing Glen's forehead. She got up and crossed the room. "I'm sure you'll feel better tomorrow." She reached up and turned off Glen's light.

Glen lay down, pulling the sheet up to his chin. He reached down for Jasper and stroked the dog's soft fur.

"I'm glad you're here, Jasper. I can always depend on you." Jasper let out a sound of contentment and snuggled closer. "Why did I let myself get my hopes up about my dad coming this summer? I should know by now how he is. I used to think that I wanted to be just like him when I grew up. But now, I'm not so sure. And how am I ever going to fix things with Jacob? I went too far this time and I wouldn't be surprised if he never speaks to me again. I miss hanging out with him."

Glen sighed, the tiredness of the day finally catching up with him. He drifted to sleep, thinking about how to apologize to Andrew in the morning.

8

Riding the Pine

Glen rode his bike down Broadview Avenue, on his way to the second game this week between the Eagles and the Woodbridge Cougars. He shook his head, thinking what a waste of time it was to come to this game when he couldn't play.

It was going to be humiliating to have to face the team. Glen parked his bike and walked carefully over to the dugout, coming up to the bench from behind. He was trying to be quiet, hoping to sneak onto the bench without anyone noticing. So far, it was working. He could hear Jacob and a few of his teammates talking.

"That's cool," Miguel was saying. "I'm sure I'll be allowed to go."

"My brother went with some friends and told me it was awesome," Michael chimed in.

Glen wondered what they were talking about. Maybe the coach was arranging a team party.

"My parents need to know how many of you guys can come so they can make arrangements for driving and stuff," Chris told the team, pushing his glasses up on his nose again.

"I wish my parents would have my birthday party at Playdium," Marco sighed. "I can't wait to try the new video games and the go-carts."

Playdium! Glen had been dying to go there all summer. Even though he had been in some trouble this summer, he was sure his parents would let him go.

"Have you invited Glen?" Jacob asked.

"Glen?" Chris said, surprised at the question. "I don't know if I want him there. What do you guys think?"

Glen's mouth dropped in surprise. Why wouldn't they invite him if the rest of the team were going? Surely they didn't all hate him for what had happened.

The rest of the team had mixed reactions. Some of the guys Glen knew from school thought it was okay to include him, but those who didn't know Glen as well weren't sure.

"I really think we should invite him," Jacob said. "He is still a part of the team. The fight is between him and me, not you guys. I don't have a problem with him coming. After all, he's been my best friend for three years."

"I don't want him to come," Steve injected. "The guy's a maniac."

"I agree," Miguel said. "He just can't treat people the way he does and expect to get away with it."

"You guys don't know the whole story," Jacob pointed out. "Glen's got stuff going on at home, too."

"Why are you defending him?" Miguel asked.

Jacob shrugged and looked at the ground. "I've had some time to cool down, I guess. I think it is a much bigger deal not to invite him to the party."

"Well, it's my birthday," Chris said. "If I don't want him there, then I'm not inviting him. End of story."

Glen had been holding his breath throughout the conversation. He was pleased to hear that Jacob didn't hate him, but he was stunned that he was the only one on the team not invited to Playdium. More than ever, Glen wanted to repair his friendship with Jacob.

Glen slumped down onto the far end of the bench, not trying to be quiet anymore. The rest of the team stopped talking about the upcoming party, and a few of them nodded to Glen, including Jacob. Glen smiled back weakly, feeling sad that some of the guys disliked him that much.

Coach Johnson gathered the team around him. "I wanted to let you all know that Glen will not be playing in this game, but if we do win, he'll be playing in the championship game."

Glen could feel his face turn beet red and he stared hard at the ground. Everyone seemed unsure now about how to deal with him being there and how he might react. Steve seemed particularly timid.

"Now, let's try to put this behind us and go out there and have a great game!" The coach included Glen in his smile and everyone moved back to the bench.

Glen caught Jacob's eye, hoping his friend would come and sit with him, but Jacob was already sitting down beside Ryan.

"Play ball!" the umpire called, and the team turned their attention to the field. Glen stared at the ground, not really caring about the game. He wondered if Jacob was right about the things he had said at the pool. Maybe he had been bringing down the team's morale. He had thought he was helping to build their skills by pointing out what they were doing wrong. He shook his head.

The Eagles were the home team and Glen wondered if that would make a difference. It usually gave a team confidence to bat last. Michael was the starting pitcher, and Glen hesitantly shouted some words of encouragement.

"Come on, Michael! You can get this guy! Easy out!"

Coach Johnson glanced sharply at Glen, but smiled when he heard what Glen was yelling.

The Eagles and the Cougars were vying for the final spot in the championships, and neither team wanted to lose. Everyone was on their toes in the field and it was quickly shaping up to be a pitchers' duel.

By the end of third inning, the score was tied at 2. Coach Johnson made three substitutions, hoping to shake things up a little. Ryan went in to pitch for Michael, Maurice went into left field for Chris, and Steve to right for Nick. Glen hoped that the strategy would work.

Ryan came on strongly to start the fourth, going after each batter and never getting behind on the count. He managed to keep going into the fifth, but was losing his momentum in the sixth. The Eagles had added a run to their count, and they just had to hold the Cougars to win.

"Take your time, Ryan!" Glen yelled as the red-haired boy pitched to the second batter in the inning. The Eagles had managed the first out by pure luck. The Cougars' shortstop had hit the ball sharply down the first base line. Jacob had moved to stop it, but Ryan hadn't gone to cover first. Seeing there was no one on base to throw to, Jacob had been in a foot race with the runner, diving back to the bag just in time for the out.

"Don't forget to cover the bases out there, guys!" Glen called. The Eagles just had to win — he couldn't stand not being able to play one more game this summer.

Coach Johnson walked over to the bench and sat beside Glen. "It is good to see you encouraging the other players, Glen."

"I really am trying, Coach. If we win this one, I'll be playing in the final game, right?"

"If you stick with this new attitude, you will." Coach Johnson studied Glen's face. "I just hope that it is a real change, not just a way to get into my good graces again." He walked back to watch the fielders, calling Ken infield a bit.

The hitter was ahead in the count two to one. Glen could feel the sweat beading on his forehead and could imagine how it would feel to be on the mound right now. Ryan wound up and pitched, sending the ball straight across the plate. The batter got all of it, launching it towards the short side of left. Maurice went after it, but there was no getting to it. As it went over the fence for a home run, Glen's stomach sank. The Cougars had tied it up with only one out.

"Shake it off, Ryan!" Glen said, not feeling positive anymore. "We still have a chance."

Ryan glanced at the bench and Glen tried to smile at him. The rest of the guys on the bench were yelling encouragement too. Glen could see Ryan take a deep breath and try to keep calm. He managed to get the next batter to chase a ball and the final out came on a fly ball to third. But the damage had been done: the game was tied and the Eagles had to come through in the bottom half of the inning.

The mood on the Eagles' bench was grim. "Come on, guys! It's not over yet. We've got one more shot here to win. Let's do it!"

Some of the team murmured their agreement, and Jacob smiled a little at Glen. The two boys still hadn't spoken, but Glen was starting to feel that there was a chance that they might be friends again.

Ryan, Ravi, and Kamal were scheduled to bat in the sixth. Despite their best efforts, they couldn't get on base. Glen dropped his head into his hands. The score was still tied at the end of the sixth, and they were going into extra innings.

Coach Johnson gathered the boys around him on the bench. "Okay, I know it looks tough," he began, "but you guys have played a great game. No matter what happens, we've had a good year. Just try to keep it together out there. Jacob, call the plays for everyone. Now, let's go get 'em."

The boys quickly took the field. Much of the onus would again be on Ryan to pitch well. He stepped onto the mound, and Glen wished so much that he was out there instead. He would have loved the chance to win this one.

The first baseman was up to bat. Glen watched Ryan's pitching, holding his breath until each call was made. "Strike two!" he heard the umpire call. Ryan was up one to two. The batter swung at the next ball and it went just over Ravi's head on second. Glen wished they had a rover in little league for hits like that one. Ken charged in for the ball and threw it into second, keeping the runner to a single.

The catcher stepped up and Glen could see that he was nervous. "Ryan, go easy," he called. "He wants to hit." Glen knew the catcher would be swinging at almost anything. Ryan kept the ball off the plate for three pitches, and the hitter laid off of only one low ball. Glen twisted his fingers together, feeling the pressure. Ryan could get this guy, if he stuck to his guns. The next pitch came in, just catching the inside corner. The catcher swung too late. "Strike three!" called the umpire. "Batter's out!"

The left fielder's turn at bat produced a single, and with a man on first and second and one out, the pitcher came up. He and Ryan battled back and forth. On the fifth pitch, the batter was out in front of the ball, and tried to hold up. He couldn't stop in time and popped it up on a power bunt. "Infield fly! Batter's out!" were the best words Glen had heard all game!

One more out to go. Glen could see the strain in Ryan's face, but Michael had already come out of the game, and couldn't go back in to pitch. With Glen on the bench, there was no one to relieve Ryan. If only I hadn't gotten in trouble, Glen thought to himself, we would've had enough pitchers to get through this. He was beginning to see how one player could have a big impact on a team.

"Okay, guys! Big D out there now!" he shouted.

The third baseman swung at the first pitch, which was a soft one from Ryan. He hit it into the gap in right, and the runner on second tore off the base. He had a chance to come home on a hit like that! Glen jumped to his feet, yelling for Steve to get the ball and get it in. Ken, knowing that Steve couldn't throw to the infield from where he was, positioned himself to relay the ball in. Getting it from Steve, he saw the runner rounding third. Glen saw him put everything he had into the throw, and watched it streak towards home. Miguel planted himself firmly on home plate and opened his glove. The left fielder was coming in hard and it was going to be close. "Safe!" the umpire called as the ball thudded into Miguel's glove.

"Safe! He was out by a mile!" Glen shouted, losing his temper for a moment. They were so close! He quickly shut his mouth and closed his hands into fists, pounding on the screen.

Ryan now faced the shortstop with men on first and second and two out. Glen thought his heart would burst with the anxiety he was feeling. The Eagles had one last at-bat, but couldn't let the Cougars get another run. Ryan wound up and pitched. The hitter, with the adrenaline pumping from his team's run, couldn't lay off. He popped it up to left field, and Maurice ran in, easily making the play.

This was it Glen thought, this was their final shot at it all. They were at the top of the order, but with the substitution made earlier, that meant Steve was leading off the inning. Glen prayed that he could hit the ball. Once he was running, Steve had some speed.

"Wait for your pitch, Steve!" Glen called. "Make him pitch to you. You can do it!"

Steve glanced at Glen, seeming startled by the friendly advice. He stepped into the batter's box and did what Glen had instructed. It paid off in a single.

"That's it! Way to go. Everyone hits now, everyone hits!" Glen was jumping up and down in excitement. "Come on, Marco, just touch green. No heroes now, no heroes!"

Marco's thick, dark brows were pulled down in concentration. Glen couldn't stand still as he watched the count climb to three and two. Full count. Marco saw the last pitch coming all the way and made contact to send it up the middle. Steve shot for second and both runners were safe!

Maurice nervously stepped up to the plate, moving the bat around behind his head.

"Soft hands, Maurice!" Glen yelled. "Don't let him rattle you! Keep that bat still!"

Maurice swung at a pitch that was outside, dribbling it to the shortstop. Glen's heart sank. He could see the double play coming. With the force on, the runners had to go. The shortstop scooped the ball up, lobbing it easily to third to get Steve, and the third baseman fired it back to second in time to get Marco. Trying for the triple play, the second baseman threw quickly to first, hoping to get Maurice. His accuracy was off and the ball flew over the first baseman's head and out of bounds.

"Out of play!" the umpire called. "Runner take your base." He pointed to second! Glen and the Eagles were stamping their feet, cheering for Maurice, even though he had hit into the double play. On the Cougars' bench, Glen could hear groans and see the players shaking their heads. That error had put the tying run into scoring position.

Ken was dancing from one foot to the other in anticipation. Grabbing the bat tightly, he stepped up to the plate. Glen could see the tension in Ken's wiry frame. Glen hoped that Ken could keep his wits about him. "Just advance the runner, Ken! Maurice, run on anything, remember: we have two away!"

Ken swung and missed for strike one, but watched the next two pitches miss the plate for two and one. Stepping into the next offering, Ken sent it hard into the infield. As the second baseman charged in for it, the ball took a weird hop and shot off to the left, leaving him scrambling after it. It rolled to the outfield, and Maurice slid into third unchallenged.

Jacob was up next "Come on, Jacob! You can do this! Bring them home!" Glen yelled to his friend. He saw the confidence in Jacob as he stepped up to the plate.

"Be ready out there, guys!" Glen called to the runners. "Go on contact!"

With the count at one and one, Glen saw the ball leave the pitcher's hand and knew that it was the pitch Jacob always waited for. So did Jacob. Never taking his eyes off the ball, he put all his weight into his swing, getting full extension.

Crack!

The ball screamed past the infield and sent the fielders running back. Jacob had sent it to the fence between right and centre. With two out, the runners didn't wait to see if the ball would be caught; they were running as soon as they heard the sound of leather on wood. Maurice scored easily to tie it and Ken was burning up the bases. Glen saw Ken coming into third as the fielder scooped the ball and hoped the coach would send him.

Coach Johnson never hesitated. He sent Ken flying for home with the ball fast on his heels. Ken threw himself into a slide, hoping to get in under the ball. Glen heard the thwack as it slammed into the catcher's glove, but Ken was already touching the plate and there had been no tag. "Safe!" the umpire called. "Safe!"

The Eagles' bench exploded onto the field. It didn't matter that they still had a base runner — they had won! Jacob had knocked in the tying and winning runs! Glen raced onto the field with the rest of the team, but they had lifted Jacob onto their shoulders before he could congratulate his friend. He settled for whooping and clapping instead. The Eagles were going to the championships and Glen was going to get to play!

9

Box Seats

Arriving home, Glen put his bike away in the garage. Andrew's truck was in the driveway, but that didn't seem to be such a bad thing to Glen anymore. He couldn't believe that the Eagles had won! He flew up the steps and into the living room, throwing himself down in a chair.

"How was the game?" Josh asked.

"It was incredible! We won and we're going to the championships! Jacob had a really good game."

Catherine and Andrew exchanged surprised glances.

"I'm glad to hear it," Glen's mother said. "I'm so pleased you'll get to play again this summer." She paused, taking in Glen's beaming smile. "It sounds as if you coped well with your punishment." Catherine's voice was full of approval.

"Yeah, I guess so," Glen sighed. "I had a chance to think about some things."

"Well, if that's the case," Andrew began, "then I have a surprise for you." Glen's ears perked up. "One of my customers has season tickets for the Jays," Andrew explained. "He passed a pair on to me for tomorrow night's game against the Mariners. Are you interested, Glen? They're box seats."

"Box seats!" Glen exclaimed, sitting straight up. "Of course I'm interested!" Andrew's surprise had taken part of the sting out of not being invited to Playdium.

"I know you're trying to change, Glen, and I think you deserve a treat," Catherine smiled.

The family settled down to watch some television, but Glen couldn't keep his mind on the program. He was too excited about tomorrow night's Jays game at the SkyDome. Strangely enough, the thought of spending a whole evening just with Andrew didn't seem so bad. In fact, he was sort of looking forward to it. There was still a tiny part of him that felt disloyal to his dad for thinking that way, but he thought about everything that his mother and Josh had said to him: Liking Andrew didn't mean he loved his father any less. He didn't have to choose between them, and could enjoy Andrew's company without hurting his dad. Glen promised himself that he and Andrew would have a good time.

* * *

"Come on, Glen," Andrew called. "Let's get going or we'll never find parking."

"Are we driving to the game?" Glen asked, surprised. "I thought we'd be taking the streetcar. Isn't parking expensive?"

"Yeah, but let's go all out tonight!"

"Okay. Let me go and grab my glove first." Glen ran upstairs to his room. He hoped that they might have a chance to catch a ball tonight.

Climbing into the truck, Glen still felt a little nervous about the evening. It was the first time that he and Andrew were going to spend time alone. He hoped that they'd find something to talk about.

As they drove down Broadview to Queen Street, Glen began to relax as he and his stepfather talked about their favourite baseball players.

"I think Tony Fernandez is a great player," Andrew said. "He's got speed on the bags and is quick in the infield."

"Yeah," Glen replied. "But Delgado is easily the Jays' best player."

"You know, you could learn a lot from Delgado," Andrew began. "He's a real team player and a leader in the clubhouse. There are very few major league teams that name a captain, and the Jays named him as one last year. It was surprising, considering how young he is."

Glen hoped that he wasn't in for a lecture on team spirit. That would ruin the night.

"Do the Eagles have a team captain?" Andrew asked.

"No, we never elected one. It's too late in the season to do it now. But the coach will choose an MVP after the last game. I guess I blew my chances at winning."

Andrew pulled onto John Street and began scouting for parking. "Don't take it too hard, Glen. It has been a difficult summer for you, hasn't it?"

Glen nodded. "I was disappointed that my dad didn't come, and then I fought with Jacob and got benched. It was tough."

"It was hard for your mother to see you so upset about your dad," Andrew said. "We both know how much you had been looking forward to seeing him and I'm sorry it didn't work out."

Glen nodded again, but didn't reply. He didn't trust himself to talk too much about his dad.

"I hope you don't think that I've been trying to take his place," Andrew continued carefully. "Bob will always be your dad, but I do hope that you and I can be friends. He and I have talked about you and Josh. He wants you to have someone here when he can't be."

Glen bit his lip. He hadn't known that Andrew and his dad had ever spoken to each other. He supposed that having his dad okay with Andrew being here did make it a little easier. Living with Andrew was going to be different from living with his dad, but it might be all right.

"Thanks for telling me that," Glen replied. "It makes me feel better."

Turning into a parking lot, Andrew managed to get a spot. He and Glen began walking down to the SkyDome, passing the hotdog vendors on the street. Waiting to cross at the lights, Glen looked up at the SkyDome. Bursting from the building were the huge sculptures of players and umpires. They always made Glen smile.

"Try to stay with me," Andrew said as they walked up the stairs and across the bridge to the gates. He flipped a loonie to the street drummer playing at the end of the bridge.

"Thanks, man!" he called to Andrew.

There wasn't much of an opportunity to talk as they navigated their way through the crowd. It seemed to Glen as if everyone in Toronto was going to the game that night. The pair checked their tickets, found the right gate, and wound their way through the concession stands and souvenir racks down to the box seats' section.

"Wow!" Glen exclaimed. "Look how close we are! This is much better than the nosebleeds."

Andrew laughed. "The game is way better if the players are larger than ants, too."

They watched the teams warming up and Glen was again struck by Delgado's confidence on the field. He greeted all the players, even on the other team, and signed a few autographs for fans leaning over the railing by first base. The Jays were home to the Mariners and Ken Griffey Jr. would be in the outfield tonight for the Mariners. He was a great player, and Glen liked him almost as much as Delgado.

The Jays had a good team this year, with some new faces including Homer Bush, Graeme Lloyd, and Willie Greene.

David Wells had come home to the Jays and was starting the game against Jamie Moyer for the Mariners.

By the bottom of the third inning, the Jays were down 2 to 1. Delgado was oh-for, but Glen was still enjoying himself. No matter how he batted, Delgado had a ready smile for his teammates and the fans. Glen wondered how he managed not to lose his temper when errors were made.

"Are you hungry, Glen?" Andrew asked in the third inning.

"I sure am!" Glen replied enthusiastically. "Can we get some nachos and hotdogs?"

Andrew laughed. "Well, you can get both if you want, but I've got to watch what I'm eating. You stay here and I'll run and get the food. Will you be okay?"

"Yeah. Can you get me a drink too, please?" Glen never took his eyes off the field.

Nodding his head, Andrew made his way to the aisle and up to the concession stands. Glen was drinking in the atmosphere, thinking what great seats these were.

It was the bottom of the fourth by the time Andrew, weighed down with food, sat down beside Glen again.

"Wow! Was it ever crowded! I got you some extra stuff because I'm not going up there again!"

"Thanks!" Glen laughed, pleased with the choices Andrew had made.

"What'd I miss?"

Glen filled him in on what had happened in between bites of his hotdog. "Why do hotdogs taste better at the ball park?" he wondered out loud.

"I know what you mean," Andrew replied, licking his lips.

The pair continued to enjoy their meal and cheered the Jays on. By the time the seventh-inning stretch came, they were ready for it.

"Boy, even in box seats I get stiff after a while," Andrew groaned.

They followed the leaders, enjoying the movements, belting out: "Okay! Okay! Blue Jays! Blue Jays! Let's ... play ... ball!" and laughing.

In the eighth inning, Delgado came up to the plate again. This would probably be his final at-bat in the game, and he was one for three. Glen just knew he was due and kept his fingers crossed. It was 4 to 3 for the Mariners, and the Jays needed everyone to hit. With Homer Bush on second, Delgado represented the go-ahead run.

As Delgado swung on a two-and-one count, Glen heard the crack of the bat meeting the ball. Arcing high in the air, the hit had the outfielder scrambling to the wall. He and Andrew leapt to their feet.

"That's gone!" Glen cried, knowing already that it would be a homer.

"Glen, grab your glove!" Andrew shouted. "It's headed for our section."

Scrambling excitedly for his glove, Glen watched in amazement as the ball cleared the wall.

"You go for it! You're taller!" Glen shouted, quickly throwing the glove to Andrew. Standing as far back in the box as he could, Andrew leapt up and snagged the ball before anyone else could grab it. Pulling the glove safely into his chest, Andrew plucked the ball from it and tossed it carefully to Glen.

"I can't believe I have Delgado's home run in my hands!" Glen was jumping up and down in excitement. Turning around, he held up the ball for the crowd to see and their section cheered for him.

"Look, Glen!" Andrew pointed up to the Jumbotron.

Glen saw his own face beaming back at him and, without thinking, turned back and hugged Andrew. Surprised at his own reaction, Glen pulled back a little and Andrew just kept smiling. He reached over to Glen and ruffled his hair. "We'll have to put that up on the mantle at home," he said.

"I just can't believe you caught it!" Glen exclaimed. "What a great game this is! I'm so glad we're here."

"Me too," Andrew said. "Now, let's hope that the Jays can hang onto the lead."

The Jays added one more run in the eighth, and kept the Mariners scoreless in the ninth. The Jays won, topping off the evening perfectly. Heading back to the truck, Glen just couldn't keep the smile off of his face. He didn't know anyone who had ever caught a home run at a Jays' game and it had been so exciting. He wondered if Jacob had been watching the game on TV and saw him and Andrew on the Jumbotron.

Waiting in line to get out of the parking lot, Glen and Andrew relived the moment of catching that ball.

"I thought for sure it was going to go over your head," Glen said. "I didn't know you could catch like that."

"I guess I never told you that I used to play little league," Andrew replied. "We have more in common than you think."

Glen smiled. "Thanks for bringing me to the game. It was the most fun I've had all summer."

"I was glad to do it," Andrew answered. "I hope that we can do more things together now. I had a lot of fun too."

While Glen had begun the evening trying to be nice to Andrew because he had promised his mother he would, he was beginning to see Andrew in a new light. He was glad they had talked about his dad earlier, and it had been a good night. Now they had a great memento of it all, too. Glen decided to lay it all on the line.

Turning to face Andrew, Glen said, "Can I ask you some-thing?"

"Of course. Shoot."

"I was wondering if maybe you would like to come to my championship tomorrow night?"

"I would love to," Andrew replied, grinning from ear to ear. "In fact, how about if the whole family comes? You know how much Megan wants to see you play."

"Sure, that would be great." Glen sat back, pleased at how well the night had gone. Maybe he and Andrew could be friends after all.

10

New Beginnings

The day after the Jays' game, Catherine was in the back-yard gardening when Glen came downstairs for a snack in the late afternoon. He was glad to see his mom home early. Glen knew that she had been working hard this summer at her café. She had been asleep by the time he and Andrew had gotten home last night because she was opening the café this morning.

Going outside to help his mom, Glen couldn't help think-ing about the game the Eagles were playing that night against the Mississauga Panthers. Glen really wanted his team to win and be the new little league champions.

Grabbing the gardening fork, Glen knelt down beside his mom and started digging up the weeds.

"Hey, you," his mother said. "How was the game last night?"

"It was great," Glen replied. "Did Andrew tell you about the home run he caught?"

"He mentioned it this morning, but he thought you'd like to tell me about it. I've been waiting to hear about it all day."

"It was totally amazing! Delgado launched one in the eighth and it was coming right at our section. I knew that it would go over my head, so I threw Andrew my glove. He was great. How come you never told me he used to play baseball?"

"I guess it just never came up." His mom was smiling. "It sounds like you had a good time. I'm glad. Can you pass me the pruning shears, please?"

Passing them to his mother, Glen continued talking about the game. "The seats were awesome. We had so much room compared to the regular seats and I ate a ton of junk food. It was a great night."

Carefully pruning the rosebushes, Catherine said, "You and Andrew seem to be getting along better."

"Well, I guess he's not such a bad guy after all," Glen admitted. "I promised you that I would try to give Andrew a chance and I have been doing it. He's been pretty good about everything that's happened this summer and it was great that he took me to the Jays' game. I know that I was kind of mean to him before."

"I know that Andrew isn't exactly like your father," Catherine began, "but I hope that you'll come to appreciate him. I want you to know that I did love your father very much when we were married, but I love Andrew now and he has been good to all of us. No matter what has happened, he has never disappointed me."

"I know." Glen concentrated on uprooting a stubborn weed. "Josh told me a lot about what it was like when you and dad were married. I guess it has been better for you since you met Andrew."

"In some ways, yes," his mom replied. "But it has been hard to watch you be disappointed by your dad over and over again. And it was even harder to see how angry you were at Andrew."

"I was angry at him," Glen admitted. "I thought that Andrew being here was keeping Dad away, but I guess not. All the stuff that's happened this summer has changed my mind about a lot of things."

Glen began to clean up all the weeds he had pulled and dead stems that his mother had pruned, putting them in a large plastic bag.

"There's one more thing I'd like to talk to you about, Glen," Catherine said. "Just like Andrew has been trying to get closer to you and Josh, I have been trying to get closer to Megan. It may have seemed as if I was spending all of my time with her, but she is only six years old and I wanted to be sure that she was coping with the change. Megan doesn't remember her own mother and this has been a major adjustment for her."

Glen kept his eyes on the bag as he filled it. Josh had probably told her what he had said earlier about Megan stealing his mom's attention. He had been feeling some resentment towards Megan, but didn't want to admit it.

"Megan will never take your place, Glen." His mother came over and tilted his face up to look at him. "I love both you and Josh with all of my heart. But I also need to find a place in my heart for her. Can you understand that?"

Glen nodded. Deep down, he had known that his mother still loved him, but it was good to hear her say it. Tying up the bag, he walked over to his mom and gave her a kiss on the cheek.

"I'm glad we talked about this," she said, giving Glen a big hug.

"Me too," he replied. "You know that the Eagles' championship game is tonight, right? I asked Andrew last night if he would come to see me play and he said the whole family would come. Will you be there?"

"Of course, Glen," she laughed. "I wouldn't miss this game for the world."

* * *

Arriving early at the diamond that night for the game against the Mississauga Panthers, Glen's stomach was doing flip-flops. His family had dropped him off early at the diamond while they went to run some errands. He had wanted lots of time to warm up and everyone would be back for the start of the game.

Dropping his baseball bag on the bench, Glen saw Ravi coming down the hill to the diamond. Still feeling a little awkward, Glen waved tentatively. He was pleased when Ravi returned his wave.

"I guess you're looking forward to playing tonight, eh, Glen?" Ravi asked, stopping at the bench.

Glen smiled. "I sure am. But I have to admit that you guys were doing pretty good without me."

"Yeah, we were," Ravi agreed with a grin. "But it's still good to have you back."

The two boys moved onto the field and began tossing the ball back and forth. Members of both teams started to arrive a few minutes later. It seemed as if everyone was there early. Glen could feel the excitement on the diamond.

Coach Johnson arrived and gathered the team for a pre-game talk. "We've had a great season, guys, and I'm proud of you. It took a lot of work to get here and I want you to go out and enjoy this game. The starting lineup will be Marco, Chris, Jacob, Kamal, Nick, Miguel, Ken, and Ravi. Steve and Maurice, you'll be subbed in later. I want all three pitchers to take two innings each: Michael, you'll start, Ryan will take middle relief, and Glen will close. Kamal, will you go take the coin toss, please?"

"Heads!" Kamal called as the umpire flipped the coin. "Heads it is," the umpire said. "Do you want the field or the bat?"

"Field," Kamal replied. The Eagles had home-team advantage!

Sitting down on the bench, Glen glanced at the other team. The Eagles had not met the Panthers since the third week in July, but they had split the wins one each. It promised to be a good matchup. He only wished he could be on the mound for the whole game, but knew that it wouldn't be fair. He took a deep breath and tried to slow his racing heart.

Michael was looking strong during his warm-up pitches, and Glen knew that he would throw his whole heart into every pitch. With each ball Michael threw, Glen called it as it came in, trying to gauge the umpire's strike zone. It was a tight one. But as long as it stayed in the same place for both teams, they would have a chance at winning.

Michael faced six batters in the first inning, and looked a little tired by the third out. With such a small strike zone, he had pitched more than he usually had to. The damage had been minimal though, with only one run scoring for the Panthers.

Michael came off the mound rubbing his pitching arm.

"That was a tough inning," he said to Glen, taking off his baseball hat and wiping the sweat from his face. His normally spikey black hair was matted down.

"You still did a good job," Glen replied.

"Thanks, man!"

Michael smiled and for the first time Glen noticed that the other boy wore braces.

"Let's get it back, guys," Glen called to the rest of the team as they came off the field. "We've got lots of time."

Glen couldn't stay on the bench; he was just too excited. He wouldn't be in the batting order until the fifth inning, so he paced nervously up and down the fence by third base. "Take your time, Marco!" he called, as their leadoff batter took his place at the plate. The Panthers' pitcher was good, firing in strikes and going quickly through the Eagles' order.

By the end of the first, the score was tied at one all.

Glen could see that the Eagles and the Panthers were evenly matched, and runs for both teams came only with a fight. Even with the advantage of batting in the bottom half of the inning, the Eagles couldn't seem to pull ahead. Ryan didn't fare any better than Michael had.

Steve had moved into right field for Nick, and Maurice had come in to play left. Glen trotted out to the mound to warm up. He almost had to remind himself to breathe in his excitement at being back on the field.

"Play ball!" the umpire called.

The third baseman came up to the plate, and Glen closed his eyes for a second to focus his concentration. He blocked the noise from the spectators and the benches from his mind, hearing only his own thoughts telling him he could do this. Almost before he knew it, they were out of the inning. The Eagles had allowed only one run to score, and the Panthers had stranded two runners.

Through the first four innings, the score went back and forth, with the Panthers finally up 4 to 3 to start the fifth.

"Great inning," Coach Johnson said as Glen came off the field.

Steve was up first in the fifth. He connected solidly and sent the ball up the middle for a single. Glen was surprised to see the flow of Steve's swing — he had come a long way this season. Glen hoped that he might get to bat this inning, but there were still another six batters ahead of him.

He sat on the edge of the bench, studying the other pitcher. He watched for where his release point was, where he stood after a pitch, and how ready he was to react to a ball hit back to him. Glen was planning his strategy for his turn at bat. The Panthers' pitcher was good, but not as good as their first pitcher had been. The Eagles were quickly finding their rhythm and Glen kept cheering them on.

Even when Ken struck out, Glen managed to keep his frustration to himself. "That's okay," he called. "That's only one. Come on, Eagles!"

The bases were loaded when Marco smacked a double into the right-field corner, scoring Steve and Miguel and tying the game again at 5 apiece. As Ravi came into third, he was watching the base coach for the signal, and Glen could see the confusion on his face. Instead of stopping on the base, he hesitated for a moment and then started running for home!

"Ravi!" Glen shouted, but there was no turning back now. "Hard, Ravi! Go hard!"

The Panthers reacted quickly to the new threat, and threw to home. Ravi slammed on the brakes, trying to turn back. The catcher threw to third and they soon had Ravi in a rundown. Glen groaned, wondering what had possessed Ravi to keep going.

The catcher soon moved in and tagged Ravi, sending him to the bench and giving the Eagles two out. As Ravi came to the bench, he hung his head. "I'm sorry, guys," he said. "I got my signals confused. I thought the coach was sending me and I couldn't understand why, but I went anyway."

The team murmured their responses to Ravi, and he sat down dejectedly.

Glen could feel the team losing hope as they watched Maurice strike out. "Hey!" Coach Johnson called, startling Glen. "We're still tied here, guys. Let's talk it up out there and go for it! I don't want to hear anything negative from anyone!" he finished, looking at Glen.

Glen bit his lip and picked up his glove. He knew that the coach was right. It was the top of the sixth and they had one more at-bat coming. He went to the mound, determined to do what he could to help his team.

Facing the top of the order, Glen pitched fiercely, striking out the first batter. His confidence was back and he was sure that the Eagles could hold on. As a left-handed batter came up, he checked to make sure the fielders were in position before he wound up. "Strike one!" the umpire called. Glen took the ball back from Miguel, and made sure the batter was ready. He wasn't going to get called on a quick return this game!

Pitching to a full count, Glen released his last offering. The batter watched it coming, moving the bat around nervously. Glen dropped his chin to his chest as he watched the hitter lay off and the umpire call a ball. That was his first walk.

"Shake it off, Glen," he heard Nick call from the bench. "You know you can do this!"

Rubbing the ball nervously in his hands, Glen sized up the next batter. He had watched the first baseman go for the long ball in previous innings and knew he looked for an outside pitch. Motioning the fielders back, he turned to face the plate. Glen wound up, staring at the outside corner the entire time. If he could place this pitch right, he thought, he could get the guy to pop it up, even if it went deep.

Glen was right. The first baseman went after the pitch, sending it up and out to centre. Ken had lots of time to get under it and snapped his glove shut for the second out. One more to go, then it was up to the hitters.

The pitcher was up next, and Glen knew he wasn't the Panthers' strongest hitter. He decided to go after him hard, and pitched over the heart of the plate. Rather than go down looking, the batter swung wildly at the third pitch, sending it straight at second base. Ravi scooped it up and with the force on, stepped on the bag for the third out. The score remained tied.

Several guys slapped Glen on the back as they came in, and he felt like part of the team again. Jacob was leading off and Glen was batting third. Jacob seemed calm and Glen envied his steady nerves.

Jacob fouled off the first pitch and managed to lay off the next two that were just like it. He was waiting for one inside and got it. Stepping back to line it up, Jacob swung hard and sent the ball screaming down the third-base line. He tore out of the box and never hesitated at first, rounding the base and going for a double. Jacob slid into the base with time to spare and the team couldn't stop cheering. That was the way to start off an inning!

Kamal was up second and hit a sacrifice fly out to right field. As soon as it touched the fielder's glove, Jacob was charging for third. The fielder had a good arm and fired the ball in to the bag, but the third baseman missed the tag and Jacob was safe!

Glen swallowed hard and stepped up to the plate. He promised himself he would be patient and reminded himself that a walk was as good as a run; they needed the men on base. "Ball four!" the umpire called. "Batter, take your base."

Glen stood on first and could hear the blood pounding in his ears. He stared at Coach Johnson, practically willing him to call the hit-and-run. Steve was up to bat, and Glen was worried that the coach would avoid the play because Steve wasn't their best hitter. In any good hit-and-run play, the batter had to swing to protect the runner.

Glen fought hard to keep himself on the base as he watched Steve battle to a three and one count. There was only one out and the timing was perfect to call the play. Steve stepped back into the batter's box and looked at the coach. Glen's heart leapt as he saw him give the signal for the hit-and-run play.

As soon as the ball left the pitcher's fingertips, Glen was off the bag and streaking for second. Out of the corner of his

eye, he saw Steve swing and miss! The catcher came up fast
with the ball and fired. The second baseman, caught unaware,
was slow off the mark and missed the throw. As it bounced
into the outfield, Glen slid into second and saw Jacob take off
for home.

The Eagles' bench was going crazy, yelling for Jacob to
run. As Jacob touched home plate, the Eagles' bench burst
onto the field. The championship was theirs! It was chaos for
the first few minutes as the team tried to high-five everyone at
once. His teammates were telling Glen what a good play he
had made and shaking Jacob's hand. Coach Johnson tried to
restore order long enough for the two teams to shake hands.
The Panthers were good sports and congratulated the Eagles
on their win.

As the Panthers began packing up, the spectators came
onto the field to congratulate the players. Glen ran over and
gave his mom a big hug.

"I'm so proud of you, Glen!" she exclaimed.

"You were great!" Megan said, hugging him too.

Andrew and Josh clapped Glen on the back. "That was a
great play, Glen," Andrew said. "You were so fast off the mark
that the second baseman didn't know which way to go! I think
that we should go out and celebrate the victory," he announced.

"Can we go to The Peppercorn?" Glen asked eagerly, his
heart still pounding with excitement.

"Sure!" Catherine replied.

"Okay, boys, can I get you to come back here for a few
minutes?" Coach Johnson called.

Turning back to the field, Glen was surprised to see Maria
standing just off to one side. Glen had seen her with Colleen
at a few of the games, but he hadn't spoken to her since that
awful day at the pool. He was pleased that she had seen him
play in the final game.

"Hi, Maria." He hoped that she was waiting there for him.

"Hi, Glen." She smiled, looking at Glen through her long dark eyelashes. "Ryan told us you were going to be playing today. You were great out there."

"Thanks!" Glen felt like he was grinning from ear to ear.

"Well," she said with a smile, tossing her hair over her shoulder, "I've got to go, but maybe I'll see you before school starts."

As she walked away, Glen stared after her. Coach Johnson's voice broke the spell. "Get over here, Glen!" he called good-naturedly.

The team gathered around, still congratulating each other.

"Now that the season is officially over, I would like to present the award for the most valuable player. I chose the winner based not only on his excellent skills, but on his sportsmanship and leadership qualities. He was always ready to lend a hand and encourage the rest of team. Jacob, could you come over here and accept your award?"

Jacob looked surprised and stepped up amid the clapping of his teammates.

"Thanks, Coach! I can't believe it. This is totally cool!" He held the trophy up for everyone to see.

Glen was pleased that Jacob had won the award, but he couldn't help feeling just a little jealous. Glen knew that he was a better player, but he had to admit that Jacob had been a better sport and more of a team player.

As the boys began to gather their gear, Jacob hesitated, glancing at Glen. Glen still missed his friendship with Jacob and thought this would be a good time to make the first move. He walked over to Jacob, smiling.

"Congratulations, Jacob," he said shyly. "You deserve it."

"Thanks." Jacob was beaming. "You played an awesome game. It was great to have you back again."

The two boys shook hands, each pleased that they were on speaking terms again.

"Jacob," Glen began, "I wanna say that I'm sorry for everything — the argument at the pool, the way I was acting about the team, and especially for shoving you. I know I was wrong and I hope we can still be friends."

"Apology accepted." Jacob smiled at his friend. "Listen, my parents and I are going out to eat at Granby's. Do you want to come?"

Glen was relieved that Jacob seemed to have forgiven him. He hoped that, in time, they would be best friends again. But right now, he wanted to be with his own family.

"Thanks, but we're already going out." Glen jerked his head towards his family. "I've got to fill you in on everything that's happened in the last two weeks. Especially the Jays' game I went to with Andrew."

Jacob raised his eyebrows in surprise. "Sounds like you do have a lot to tell me."

Glen laughed. "We still have three weeks left before school starts," he pointed out. "Do you want to go to the pool tomorrow?"

"Sure!" Jacob said enthusiastically. "I'll call you in the morning."

The two friends exchanged smiles and hurried back to where their families were waiting.

"Hey, Glen!" Jacob called to his friend. "This time, I'll watch the lifeguard for you!"

Glen laughed and waved to Jacob, pleased that there was still some summer left for them to enjoy.

Other books you'll enjoy in the Sports Stories series...

Baseball

☐ *Curve Ball* by John Danakas #1
Tom Poulos is looking forward to a summer of baseball in Toronto
until his mother puts him on a plane to Winnipeg.

☐ *Baseball Crazy* by Martyn Godfrey #10
Rob Carter wins an all-expenses-paid chance to be batboy at the
Blue Jays' spring training camp in Florida.

☐ *Shark Attack* by Judi Peers #25
The East City Sharks have a good chance of winning the county
championship until their arch rivals get a tough new pitcher.

Basketball

☐ *Fast Break* by Michael Coldwell #8
Moving from Toronto to small-town Nova Scotia was rough, but
when Jeff makes the school basketball team he thinks things are
looking up.

☐ *Camp All-Star* by Michael Coldwell #12
In this insider's view of a basketball camp, Jeff Lang encounters
some unexpected challenges.

☐ *Nothing but Net* by Michael Coldwell #18
The Cape Breton Grizzly Bears face an out-of-town basketball
tournament they're sure to lose.

☐ *Slam Dunk* by Steven Barwin and Gabriel David Tick #23
In this sequel to *Roller Hockey Blues*, Mason Ashbury's basketball team adjusts to the arrival of some new players: girls.

☐ *Courage on the Line* by Cynthia Bates #33
After Amelie changes schools, she must confront difficult former
teammates in an extramural match.

☐ *Hockey Heat Wave* by C.A. Forsyth #27
In this sequel to *Face Off*, Zack and Mitch encounter some trouble when it looks like only one of them will make the select team at hockey camp.

☐ *Shoot to Score* by Sandra Richmond #31
Playing defence on the B list, alongside the coach's mean-spirited son, are tough obstacles for Steven to overcome, but he perseveres and changes his luck.

Riding

☐ *A Way With Horses* by Peter McPhee #11
A young Alberta rider invited to study show jumping at a posh local riding school uncovers a secret.

☐ *Riding Scared* by Marion Crook #15
A reluctant new rider struggles to overcome her fear of horses.

☐ *Katie's Midnight Ride* by C.A. Forsyth #16
An ambitious barrel racer finds herself without a horse weeks before her biggest rodeo.

☐ *Glory Ride* by Tamara L. Williams #21
Chloe Anderson fights memories of a tragic fall for a place on the Ontario Young Riders' Team.

☐ *Cutting it Close* by Marion Crook #24
In this novel about barrel racing, a talented young rider finds her horse is in trouble just as she is about to compete in an important event.

Roller Hockey

☐ *Roller Hockey Blues* by Steven Barwin and Gabriel David Tick #17
Mason Ashbury faces a summer of boredom until he makes the roller-hockey team.

Running

☐ *Fast Finish* by Bill Swan #30
  Noah is a promising young runner headed for the provincial finals when he suddenly decides to withdraw from the event.

Sailing

☐ *Sink or Swim* by William Pasnak #5
  Dario can barely manage the dog paddle, but thanks to his mother he's spending the summer at a water sports camp.

Soccer

☐ *Lizzie's Soccer Showdown* by John Danakas #3
  When Lizzie asks why the boys and girls can't play together, she finds herself the new captain of the soccer team.

☐ *Alecia's Challenge* by Sandra Diersch #32
  Thirteen-year-old Alecia has to cope with a new school, a new stepfather, and friends who have suddenly discovered the opposite sex.

Swimming

☐ *Breathing Not Required* by Michele Martin Bossley #4
  An eager synchronized swimmer works hard to be chosen for a solo and almost loses her best friend in the process.

☐ *Water Fight!* by Michele Martin Bossley #14
  Josie's perfect sister is driving her crazy but when she takes up swimming — Josie's sport — it's too much to take.

☐ *Taking a Dive* by Michele Martin Bossley #19
  Josie holds the provincial record for the butterfly, but in this sequel to *Water Fight*, she can't seem to match her own time and might not go on to the nationals.

☐ *Great Lengths* by Sandra Diersch #26
  Fourteen-year-old Jessie decides to find out whether the rumours about a new swimmer at her Vancouver club are true.

Track and Field

☐ *Mikayla's Victory* by Cynthia Bates #29
Mikayla must compete against her friend if she wants to represent her school at an important track event.